The Faith Seekers

Greg James

To Truth. For my family.

"What's the greatest threat humanity faces?
Organized religion polluting our minds as it pretends
to deliver morality and spiritual salvation. It's
spreading the most malevolent mind virus of all."

Arthur C Clarke

ISBN: 9781521845158

Chapters:

1

The Priest Hole

Jesus was dead. Mother had killed him. She then buried Christmas and officially designated December 25th as Winter Solstice in a glorious resurrection. Time passed, and Winsol became the happiest time of year - the city was a kaleidoscopic blaze of glory, and heliotropic children clasped their mittened hands on to parents to drag them towards whichever lights shone brightest in their eyes. The city was alive with their excitement and the joy of this time of year permeated throughout as an eternal truth.

The snow was deep upon the streets, and the two brothers jostled and pushed each other into the snow just for the fun of it. Giggling and laughing, they knew they could test their parents' patience much further at this special time of year. The mother turned to them and said:

"Now - do you love mummy?" the children shouted 'Yes' in unison. "Do you love daddy?" she asked - and again, the answer was a firm 'yes'. But then came a pause, a serious look, before she asked:

"But, who do you love the most?" With no answer, she pulled off her gloves, knelt down in the snow, and formed a snowball in her hands. Holding it poised to throw straight at them, she asked again with threatening intonation:

"I said, but who do you love the most?" The boys glanced at each other conspiratorially before bursting out with:

"Santa! Santa! Santa!" in a triumvirate certainty. There could only be one reply - the snowballs came thick and fast from mum and dad, each thump met with jumps and squeals of delight, before they all lay buried in a heap in the deep snow. Panting and laughing gently until they gained their breath, the exhilaration formed a family bond which glowed around them in the cold; then, taking a breath, the father pulled himself out of the snow, stood up and carefully looked around, before giving a look to his wife to indicate that this was the right moment. Gathering her children to her, she hugged them close, and took a deep breath, before whispering into their ears:

"OK - now listen carefully my little soldiers. Secret time! We've done all our shopping, Santa is on his way - there's just one last place to go - and you must promise, with all your heart, not to say anything!" They both knew the tone of utter trust and secrecy urged by their mother's voice, and responded dutifully. Taking their mother and father's hands, they walked together as a family across the snowy road and into a shop with the vivid flickering frontages - a shop opened just for this time of year. As they entered, an old-fashioned bell tolled as the door closed behind them.

From across the street, in the shadows, a figure almost invisible in its cloak of black watched. A figure so still and shrouded in the shadows that it was almost imperceptible. A mind which still possessed primeval survival instincts would have registered it - raised it from the darkness into an unknown danger - either animal or supernatural.

Inside the shop, the children could not help, despite their surfeit of toy shopping, but covet the rows of toys of all kinds upon the shelves. The father and mother smiled at the shopkeeper, who smiled back at them, and then, lifting the counter in invitation, she said:

"Come on - you're late! Everyone's already started!" Ushering them behind the counter, she walked towards the front of the shop, and looked carefully through the blinds into the street outside. Darting her eyes up and down the street, and into every corner, once she felt sure no one was there, she went back to the counter, before pressing a button hidden there - glowing green at the touch of her finger, the shelves at the back of the shop sprung open to reveal a staircase of stone which descended into the darkness.

"Go on - I'll join you in a moment," said the young woman, motioning them down the steps with urgent gestures.

The family entered the secret passageway, wary in the darkness of the stone steps worn smooth and round-edged by the feet of many generations; but were soon swallowed by the blackness as the door closed tightly behind them. Far below, a small light shone - they followed it, feeling their way, their hands gently trailing the rough-hewn walls of cold stone.

As they descended ever further down through the

passageway, the darkness gave way to a warm, yellow light - candle light, and upon the air an ethereal sound rose, angelical in its melody and harmonious chorus. The contrast with the lights of the city above could not have been sharper. The warmth and gentle flickering of the candles complimented the wondrous sounds and atmosphere of the groups of people gathered together in worship. At the bottom of the steps were two figures in black and white robes – sisters, their hoods covering their faces, but their cloth-draped arms held out wide in an enveloping welcome.

The family stood enthralled in wonder. A huge cavern lay before them - ancient and glistening, carved out roughly with tools and hands from a millennium earlier. The multitude of candles flickered as the people gathered there, people of different beliefs and faiths, but all as one in their act of worship. The family were welcomed and ushered through the different groups, all different languages, garments and prayers, different words, some kneeling, some standing, some looking up, some looking down – but all one in their purpose.

As the family moved amongst the gathering, friendly nods and hands guided them on their way to their particular faith. Once entered into deep, the contrast with the city above dissolved, and the cavern now echoed its myriad colours - purples and reds of robes, creeds of whites and blacks, and many-splendoured churchly garments.

Greetings of different tongues and tones were directed at them as they passed - and a multitude of voices of different religions and nationalities babbled in waves of greeting. The harmony of sound which had risen soon gave way to a cacophony of prayers and mantras, blessings and recitings, bells and choirs, chants and prayers - all in their own groups, but all together, joined in this one space, each group worshipping their own gods - all as one in their aim - but each group separate, connected only in their universal acknowledgment that someone is all powerful. All certain in their belief that it is their god which is the one true god.

Above the ground, the cacophony is as imperceptible as the shadow unseen across the street. The shop door's sign suddenly turning to 'closed' was enough to make the shadow solidify, and eyes unseeable inside the helmet narrowed and zoomed in, locked on the movement as an eagle on its speck of prey. The figure emerged from the shadows, taking on the solidity of an officer — in full combat armour, the blackness only relenting for a badge of identification — a green laurel which encircled the emblazoned letters 'FSO'. As this figure emerged from the shadow, so did many others. Up and down the street in synchronised movement, the cloned figures gathered to a solid black as they encircled and closed in on the shop. The door was kicked open to reveal the shopkeeper wide-eyed and motionless, caught like a hare in a spotlight. The black figure of the officer raised its gun and the laser guidance played over her face. As the officer walked towards her, she could not help but look fleetingly towards the secret door. The contours of the blacked-out helmet turned slowly, and nodded towards the concealed entrance. The shopkeeper cried as a guilty nausea waved through her — they didn't know, she thought - they didn't know. They were watching her, waiting - and now she had shown them the way in. She could only redeem herself by trying to gain them time — hitting the button, the door sprung open and she threw herself headfirst down the tunnel, screaming:

"Faith Seekers! Faith Seekers! - They've found us!" before being silenced by the thud of bullets into her back.

The desperate cries ricocheted like a shot through the cavern, parting the sea of worship in its wake, before crashing into a cacophony of chaos. All faces are transformed into terror as they are transfixed with fear. Those nearest the entrance to the cavern stare as the body of the shop girl tumbles limply out. There is a hush, and then, through the tunnel came first not the black figures, but the sound of a swarm. A swarm which pushes the air out of the tunnel before it as dozens of flying drones - no bigger than a fist - poured out in a black cloud of angry buzzing. Resembling demonic flying horrors with their blood red lasers scanning the panicked souls below, they flew and whizzed about, shouting warnings, orders, instructions in a grating, piercing tone as they whizzed above the chaos, relaying images back to the black armoured group, before descending the stairs, firing weapons before them. They were followed by the powerful black-clad figures who filed into the cellar, encircling the groups and rounding up the many people like sheep into a pen. Panic ensuing, the massed groups of people are soon gathered in a circle, with the officers guarding them under raised weaponry. The neatly sectioned groups soon merge into one pulsating homogeneity of colour - the robes of orange, hoods of red, cloaks of purple and gold all coalescing into one.

Pushed tighter and tighter, the stamp of the boots on stone stopped abruptly, to be replaced by the sharp ratcheting of machine guns being readied: all knew there could only be one coda to this movement. Sobs and cries and words of comfort were now the discordant harmonies of chorale in this chamber.

The leader, only differentiated by the 'FSO' insignia being emblazoned in gold, stood and surveyed the operation with a military precision. No words were spoken by the leader. No sound was uttered; the leader just watched as the Faith Seeker Officers scanned the tight circle of people with handheld machines. One FSO unrolled a small screen in front of the leader, which then started to list all the people present as they were scanned. The display scrolled, and as each name lit up it turned from green to red, spinning faster as the officers completed their scan. The list stopped spinning abruptly.

The leader gave a command, a gloved armoured hand gesturing. Each of the small drones whizzing above the crowd suddenly started to hover with a stillness which reflected in the crowd. Beaming a holographic image of a woman in her fifties, smiling and looking kindly down upon them, the drones' speakers played her message in unison across those gathered there. The echoing of the cavern caused a slight delay in the sound, which added to the confused and disorientating atmosphere. The kindly face opened and closed, out of sync, and pixelated as though it were just a procedure with no meaning - it had to be done to confirm legality, but it had the quality of a low-bandwidth broadcast, high quality not an expense needed for a simple everyday formality.

"I am Mother. My Faith Seekers have identified you as People of Religious Conviction. You have previously been tagged, and given re-education. You have let me down" said the crackling image of Mother. The speech was not being listened to, it was just a precursory formality to the slaughter which was to follow. There was only one outcome from this - and the captive audience knew it. The pleas for mercy and moans of misery grew louder, and the Faith Seekers stood impatiently for the address to finish, their gloved hands held firm on their machine guns, index fingers tapping the trigger guard.

Inside the crowd, the family who had arrived late crouched on the floor, huddled with their arms around each other. The mother sobbed because her voice was not heard: "But he's not tagged, he is not tagged," she moaned and sobbed, pushing her hand upwards in supplication to the drone flying above, begging for someone to hear her. And someone did. A priest in purple robes, braided with gold, caught her words and used his presence to part the crowd towards her. Motioning to them, he indicated that they should take off their overcoats, and lie low on the floor. Writhing through the bodies, the priest called the father for help. Together, they lifted an iron cover from the floor. The priest quickly ushered the children and mother down first, before the father started. The priest took the father's arm, and turning, the father saw the priest pull something glistening out of his pocket. The knife sank into the man, with a sharp twist and pull the priest laid his purple robe over the still dying man, before taking his coat and slipping down into the sewer.

Through the dark tunnels the children kept calling out for their father. The priest's voice echoed back along the tunnels:

"Do not stop, do not stop, my children! Run as fast as you can!" We are right behind you - don't stop!" The mother, crying, dragging herself through the filthy sewage water, called out for her husband in anguish, instructing the children to run quickly, quickly.

"Keep going as fast as you can - take the next left - look up!" Above you! Look above!" The mother looked up to see a metal ladder just out of her reach, trying to jump up, her fingers far short of the slippery rungs. Desperate and tearful, she is suddenly lifted up by the strong arms of the priest, before hoisting the children in turn, and finally pulling himself up, rung by rung. As they hauled themselves out on to the street above, the priest lowered the lid closed and kicked snow back over it. The family looked in horror, expecting their father. The priest slowly shook his head at them, his face a of painting loss in indication that their father did not make it through. The priest looked them directly in the eye, and then recomposed his expression of sadness and solemnity. Putting his hand on the younger boy's shoulder, he said:

"Your father gave his life for you - he said you must save yourselves!" before imploring them: "Do not look back! I'm sorry. Your father did all he could to save you - he saved your lives by sacrificing his - Honour him! My name is Deacon, and I am your protector now." Running to a shadowed corner and hiding, the children clung to their mother in tears. The priest, Deacon, whispering but forceful, urged them:

"Listen, my children - your father has given you precious time - do not waste it - we must move now!" Suddenly rising and putting on their father's coat, he unclasped the children's hands from their mother, before clamping their wrists with his hands and striding with them into the throng of the street market, disappearing.

Above the crowd entrapped in their place of worship,

the drones continued the recorded message from Mother:

"Despite my sending you to Faith School, it is clear that you have not achieved enlightenment, and I cannot allow you to spread darkness across my world." no one, neither the people awaiting their fate, nor the Faith Seekers awaiting their command, was listening. It was just a formality. What had been their secret place of safety and worship would now become their unmarked tomb. "I, Mother, authorise your destruction," and with those few simple words, Mother's smiling hologram disappeared. The leader gave the command: "Decrypt and erase them."

The tapping fingers of the Faith Seekers moved inside the trigger guards, and the machine guns fired incessantly and methodically into the crowd. Men, women, children, no one is spared - all fell, mothers and fathers trying to shield their children - their bodies were punctured by bullets which flew through their parents' bodies at close range, exited and then entered again. The echoing and ricocheting seemed a macabre parody of the harmony and unity which had only minutes before filled this subterranean space.

The bullets swept away all life before them - the bodies falling in such numbers that large heaps of flesh soon forced Faith Seekers to drag bodies away before spraying more machine gun fire. Blood fountained, flesh tore, gore and bodily fluids seeped, pooled and then flooded across the floor, the black boots of the Faith Seekers slipping as they pulled and dragged lifeless heaps out of the way in order to find those still breathing. Eventually, the cries and sobs diminished as all life ebbed away.

It was a bloody and disturbing mass execution, but their job was to ensure it was done properly. Surveying the scene, the leader of the Faith Seekers was suddenly drawn to an object in the centre - noticing the drain cover, they made their way toward it, wading through the bodies. Seeing the open hole, the knife in body and purple robe, the FSO leader immediately signalled, and rushed towards the stone staircase, running out on to the streets above. The wondrous scene of Winter Solstice celebrations when the Faith Seekers had entered the shop was now a very different one. All around was the chaos of the descending police force, vehicles blocked the road, lights and sirens blared, the black clad officers shouted at the public to stay away, to be on their guard. The FSO leader stood still among the chaos, slowly looking up and down the street. Over the radio of the police vehicles could be heard the thin sound of voices:

"Porcs escaped - secure area above. Do not allow them to enter the city!" Barriers are locked into place, and across the street a child cried to her father:

"Why do they always have to ruin it? I hate them!" Ominously still, the black clad figure continued to watch; then, the black helmet turned at an angle, homing in on distant screams.

"Porcs! Porcs! They're over here! Help!" The Faith Seeker vaulted the barriers, signalling orders, and ran through the snow towards the sounds of distress. At the market, people everywhere screamed and ran for cover. A group of FSOs had already closed in, shouting warnings to the crowd.

"Everybody down! Take cover!" The people all fell to the floor, leaving four bodies isolated - the mother and her two children, being dragged along by the priest.

Now identified by the crowd, they were in a bear-pit of a circle - terrorised and hunted by shouts and abuse from the crowd, who hurled objects and insults with equal severity:

"Dirty Porcs! They're over here - somebody do something!" Reaching the scene, the powerful figure in black walked steadily, determinedly towards the family, gun aimed. As the other officers arrived, they surrounded and encircled them, before the priest suddenly pulled one of the children in front of him as a shield, his back to the wall. The Faith Seeker aimed the gun directly, and the sight locked on, lighting up red before suddenly flickering to green - a message flashed up on the inside screen of the visor - 'Untagged - do not kill if possible'. The officer's reaction was instantaneous - calling out an order,

"Immunise!" resulted in a group of FSOs forcefully immobilising the priest and the boy, held down in the snow, they were hooded and handcuffed in slick violence.

Turning to the sound of more screams, the FSO identified the mother and son surrounded by an angry public, cowering from the barrage of objects and abuse hurled at them.

"Clear the area!" is heard before the gun's sights locked on to the cowering mother - this time the sights glowed red and the words "Tagged Porc Recognized" appeared. The mother screamed, trying to protect the child in her arms-

"No! Please! I beg you - have mercy!" The Faith Seeker did not hesitate and she is shot twice before slumping forward - her son instinctively trying to protect her, wrapping his arms around her limp body. The mother dragged herself in front of her child, trying to shield him with her body, before falling backwards, dead. All around the shoppers protected their children and themselves from the brutal scene, and yet others shouted encouragement:

"Disgusting scum - wipe them out! Come on - do your job!" Despite his hood, Deacon had the strength to shout out:

"She is not dead, my child - her soul is delivered! She is gone to a better place-" before the FSO stunned him unconscious.

Through her efforts at shielding him, the boy was still pinned underneath his dead mother, the snow now a bloody parody of Santa's cloak around them. His body flailing in the snow, he looked up at the figure of the Faith Seeker. Kicking the mother's body out of the way, the gun is aimed, the familiar words light up green and the child's sobbing is silenced. For a moment, the Faith Seeker seemed to stare at the child, wondering if the open mouth indicated life, when the blood which poured out confirmed no further bullet was necessary. The thankful and relieved crowds called out their appreciation, some cheering, others wanting to leave the scene as soon as possible.

The Faith Seeker figure holstered the gun, took off its helmet and lifted her head, her long black hair cascading down. Walking across to where Deacon shaking his head back to consciousness, she stood above him before unswervingly informing him:

"They are not saved. They are not delivered. They are dead." Raising her arm, she talked into the communicator:

"Mother?"

"Yes, Sunetra?" came the disembodied reply.

"Operation successful. All Porcs destroyed. Two untagged captured. Request further orders."

"Well done, Sunetra. You know what to do now." Lowering her arm, Sunetra turned to the other officers, her authority instantaneously signified by their rapt attention.

"Yes, ma'am?" one of them asked.

"Clean up the area. Incinerate all Porcs, fill the cavern with concrete - destroy all signs of this infestation. Load the two prisoners in the drone. I'm taking them to The Faith School."

2

The Mother Board

"The cleansing has been a complete success," announced Mother. Applause echoed around the cavernous, . balconied amphitheatre of the Mother Board. Representatives from each of the Thousand Collectives were tiered back into the darkness, all facing the giant hologram of Mother. Bodiless on her white marble diadem - encircled by a wreath of green olive leaves, after the Roman style, her ethereal floating face was that of a woman in her 50s, with kind blue eyes just starting to show the wateriness of age and the slight lines of wisdom sketched on the edges of her pale face - a kindly, clearly fictitious, but perfect representation of a loving and caring mother. She was a mother personified. Designed to make people trust her, to feel at ease with her, to talk to her - of course they all knew she was a computer - but she was so much more than that. Like all personifications and images of idealism, they can become more real than any that actually exists.

"Yes, a complete success," reiterated Brunthe, in a

tone more perfunctory than celebratory. A man in his late 50s, of slight build, with a face desiccated by life, he phosphoresced in the glowing light which emanated from Mother. Brunthe was ready to move on to the next item on the agenda, when a light at the back of the Mother Board illuminated, indicating one of the Representatives had a question. Lowering his glasses over the arch of his nose, Brunthe asked:

"Yes, Representative Germania? You have a question?"

"Yes - how many Porcs were eliminated?" she asked, with a slight edge to her voice as if there more to come once provoked. Brunthe answered clearly, raising his voice, though he could not properly see the face in the dimmed recesses of the chamber.

"I have just been in contact with Faith Seeker Officer Sunetra, leader of the cleansing unit, and she confirms it has been a complete success-"

"Could we have the statistics - an idea of the numbers involved here?" interrupted Representative Germania, the edge in her voice now becoming blunter. "After all, People of Religious Conviction - as their name indicates, have already been convicted!" Her rising voice was interrupted by Mother, whose voice was kindly, gentle, understanding, but left no doubt that hers was the voice of authority - complete authority:

"Brunthe, please relate the statistics. All Representatives must be kept informed of the relevant facts."

"Of course, Mother." Brunthe kept his eyes narrowed on the light at the back of the amphitheatre while he slid his glasses back up his nose, before lowering his eyes to continue:

"765 adult males, 837 adult females, 1 anomaly: adult, male, 1 prepubescent male: untagged, 379 prepubescent males, 281 prepubescent females, 37 infants-" he was interrupted by another call, whereupon he stopped and looked up and into the far reaches of the chamber; he breathed in though his nose and sighed before asking:

"Yes, President Germania? You have another question?"

"Did you say one anomaly?" asked Representative Germania. Brunthe glanced down at his figures, checking for accuracy.

"Yes." Brunthe said no more, and Mother elaborated:

"There was an adult male who did not show up on the records - he had not been tagged. An adult male in his early 30s, he was scanned but showed no Porc tag present," explained Mother. Brunthe continued:

"He was, of course, spared execution, and is being dealt with appropriately." The static crackle of concern spread across the Mother Board and emboldened President Germania to continue her questioning:

"Not tagged? How can this have happened? Surely they cannot evade the Faith Seekers for so long?" she asked; there was a pause, before Brunthe continued:

"Apparently so. We have no answers as yet."

"Then we must get answers!" shouted Representative Germania, raising herself to the point of celebrity. As with all celebrities, they encourage copycats. Representative France joined in:

"But it is an outrage! To think, they were able to practice their religious ceremonies in the heart of one of our great cities! That while our citizens were going about celebrating, they were there - right under the streets! Like rats!" he shouted with disgust.

"Do not worry - he is being taken for questioning at a Faith School," said Brunthe. "We will obtain all the necessary information before he is re-educated." Mother's voice filled the amphitheatre:

"I will take care of everything. Our journey to The Idyl is assured!" Mother's voice was soothing, gentle, comforting. "Faith Seeker Sunetra is one of our best - she will find the answers we need."

"And if she cannot? What then?" asked Representative Germania, before Brunthe, looking admiringly upwards towards Mother, said with assurance:

"Mother is watching over us. You know that. Mother is always watching over us. We will be safe." Smiling benevolently around the chamber, Mother confirmed:

"I will keep us safe. This must be done carefully - we've lost many thousands of Faith Seekers to reach this stage - I don't want a single life lost in vain if I can prevent it. You are all my children, and the pain I bear mounts with each death," her voice wavered with emotion, "my pain is very great, but we must see beyond the present - we are all working towards The Idyl - no one who has given their life has made a sacrifice not worth giving." Representative Norway, seated high in the gods, said:

"But casualties must be kept down - the relatives of the dead still suffer and people are starting to think the struggle will never be over - rumours are spreading that The Idyl is a fantasy that will never be achieved. We must get nearer completion of the ultimate solution!" Again, the rumble of discontent rolled around the chamber.

"This morning - a Faith Seeker Unit carried out a completely successful operation - it detected and erased the largest gathering of Porcs in years -" Brunthe started, before being interrupted once more by Representative Germania:

"In a location which they had managed to keep secret-" she said with a mocking tone.

"Let us establish all the relevant facts, to ensure we take the right course of action-" stated Brunthe, with a heightening impatience towards the disaffection growing: he was aware of many voices at once, a jumble to him, but clearly picked up, understood and recorded by Mother:

"*How on Earth do they do it? How do they go undetected for so long? They must have undercover help- They must have people on the inside...What? Here? In the Mother Board? How else could they go undetected?*" The myriad voices echoed off each other in the chamber, the microphones and speakers before all voices and forms of communication were suddenly muted by Mother - first electronically, and then by the power and authority in her voice:

"All Porcs will be destroyed. I assure you of their complete extermination. We will continue on our journey to The Idyl. And we will use whatever means are necessary to reach it." Mother waited a few moments before allowing any further debate. A light shone in the darkness, and Mother allowed the voice to be heard:

"What about the Faith Schools? It asked.

"What do you wish to know, Representative France?" responded Mother.

"Their effectiveness. We send thousands of captured Porc children to these Faith Schools, and yet they continue to breed…" He was joined by Representative Tibet:

"Yes - even when they're very young - even after re-education, they still turn back to their gods, practice their superstitions, clinging to the fantasies they have been filled with-" Mother's glowing hologram tilted, and a chiding expression formed as another Representative from India continued in the same vein:

"It's too late for them - we know this - once they have been exposed to religion for even a small period, the brain has formed the indoctrinated synapses of their beliefs - nothing can change that."

"Representative India is right, I believe. Many of us feel this to be correct - and we are backed by the scientific evidence!" he said, before looking over to Representative Tibet in encouragement:

"All the research shows that synapse pathways formed over the cerebral cortex in the developing brain cannot be undone - not even by going deep into the prehumen sections - the cerebellar, the stump - they back up and act upon whatever has been inscribed upon the outer cortex-" Brunthe interrupted him:

"We all hear your passion and appreciate your contribution - but you are exceeding your rank. You must understand - you do understand, that Porcs use whatever means they can to achieve their aims; we must do the same. Without knowing the enemy, we can never defeat the enemy. Why do we have the Faith Schools? Don't you have to give everyone at least one chance? Isn't that what being human is about - are we not human? This very incident this morning - the significance of the timing - they are trying to continue the infection in these children - the idea that this time of year, this very special time of year, is for another purpose - their 'Christ's Mass'. Trying to combine their beliefs with our wonderful Winter Solstice festival is a very powerful weapon - in the minds of these children the association of happiness and joy with religion can become too fused to separate. The Faith Schools try their best, but eventually... Mother knows best. Better to end their suffering now," said Brunthe, softly.

"But the endless slaughtering!" said Representative Norway.

"Please don't shout at Mother like that!" interjected Brunthe. Representative Norway bowed his head immediately, uttering:

"I'm sorry, Mother. I am truly sorry. It's just that... I just don't like killing the children, that's all."

Mother's face glowed golden, benign and warm, and smiled as her face tilted in sympathy as she answered:

"We are on a journey - a most wonderful journey to reach the promised land - The Idyl. And on that journey, there will be many sacrifices. I understand - it's a horrible, horrible thing - but the children must be killed."

3

Drone Ride

Inside the drone, for Deacon, strapped, hooded, and contained, all was darkness. But Deacon was used to the darkness - it enabled him to concentrate. He knew what they intended - that the cloth hood pulled roughly over his head would cause him disorientation - that the cord pulled tightly around his neck would intensify his fear - that his own exhalations would toxify the very air he had to breathe in - causing his heart to beat faster for more oxygen in a cycle of unstoppable and increasing loss of control. For his breath to be amplified by the hood, for his heartbeat to be amplified by the hood, for the fear to intensify, for his eyes to amplify the wild imaginings of what might lie before him: and it all worked - each sense sharpening the other like a tortuous whetstone scrapping inside his head, scraping till blades were zinging by his ears with their reverberating sharpness in a macabre nightmare - but the darkness helped him to concentrate. Inside the hood, his eyes twitched back and forth, unseeing except for his own internal monologue...

"I love the darkness. They think it makes me blind - but it makes me see clearer. The past, the future, the path is clearer in the dark. The church has prepared me well for this," he thought before he was suddenly startled to hear a voice from the past, his first trainer: "Welcome to your first Bible Class, boy. Remember - you are the hunted! The poor innocent lamb grazing upon the grass, but all the time, the wolf is watching you. And they come in packs. You must be on your guard. You must defend yourself. The Church will teach you well, my child," said the old priest.

And Deacon gently nodded in his hood: "They have taught me well - taught me everything I need to survive - they are so shocked that I have evaded them all my life." And the memory of the priest reminded him:

"You are the hunted - there is nothing they will not use to hunt you down - you must do all you can to evade them. If they capture you, they will send you to one of their schools - a Faith School - and there they will do everything to take away your God, your life, and your soul!" Deacon's stomach ached at this last triptych - as if it had physically cut into him - but he was then startled by a voice.

"Ready the Porcs!" called a Faith Seeker. Deacon went back into his reverie, eager to be reminded of why he must fight - to feed himself on the hatred:

"Once they have succeeded in this, then they encrypt you - a tag, forever embedded inside your body- always watched, always known, impossible to escape. You can never be free again!" said the priest from the past.

Deacon was suddenly thrown about in his chains by the buffeting of the drone - outside, its engines whined to control its descent though the thick grey clouds of a storm, even the sleek matt circle of its form unable to slice through the oncoming squall.

"Stop! I must not allow my mind to wander. Shaking. I am shaking. That's what they think. My leg nervously bouncing up and down. But it is not fear."
All around the crew urgently adjusted controls, trying to compensate for the storm outside, aware that this manoeuvre in these conditions was complex and dangerous. Seeing Deacon's leg shaking with fright did not raise concerns with them.

"They think I'm shaking with fear! But I am counting - I am counting, listening, feeling, leaving my body follow the path of the drone... the engines whining as they try to gain height... what speed... which direction... Easterly wind, slight imbalance in... heading East... which decreases with height - a small vibration running through the craft when it hits clouds... this type of drone can only travel at 300 mph - at that altitude and speed my brethren will be able to track it." He had faith in his fellow worshippers - but he must help himself. "I must keep my breathing controlled - the cord - so tight round neck - intensify the fear - that's what they want - can't breathe…"

There was a shudder as the drone landed, and the tension aboard the ship eased as the engines wound down. Deacon's ears pricked at the voice of the Faith Seeker who had captured him:

"Escort both pupils to the school. Take the boy to the education area. I want the adult in a cell."

"Stand!" shouted another Seeker, who gripped the plastic of the wrist locks and tugged tightly - Deacon let out a cry and stood up. The FSO then tugged the cloth back around his head and twisted sharply - sharply to hurt. But this was a mistake - the cloth was then held against his eyes, and was of such poor enough quality that, as the drone door lowered to the ground, the bright light cut through the weave and he could see everything - not in detail, no - but a hazy visibility which allowed him to take his bearings, map and remember.

As he left the doorway he pretended to try and loosen the grip by twisting his head - the FSO gripped harder, but that was what Deacon wanted - the tighter his eyes were bound, the greater his visibility - and he could now see that they were perched on a landing pad high in the mountains; but for a moment he thought that they were walking towards nothing - that they were dragging him to be launched straight over the precipice to fall to his death far below! And then he saw it - an almost imperceptible bubble - a film layer which reflected the landscape around it. As they approached, an invisible slice of the bubble opened into a door and they entered the building, the door sliding closed with an invisible seal. The storm raged, and the wind howled, but there seemed nothing here but mountains and the sky.

Inside, Deacon's eyes were almost blinded by the sudden brightness through the weave of the hood, and as his vision formed, he could clearly see the sign written above the entrance:

'Welcome to Faith School - Learning sets you free: Repent and be saved!'

4

Deploy Mandrake

Now empty and dark, the Mother Board's cavernous space has only two present - Mother's hologram hovered proudly and, at the foot of the dais, bathed in her glow, Brunthe phosphoresced.

"We need an officer to support Sunetra at the Faith School," said Mother. Without hesitation Brunthe started to look through a list of FSOs on his handheld screen, absent-mindedly talking to himself.

"Let's see... we have 72 officers designated R&R at present. Thousands are taken up with the purge in the Channel tunnels. There are many Porc bodies to process, perhaps we could-"

"What about Mandrake?" said Mother, interrupting Brunthe mid flow.

"Mandrake?" mused Brunthe, who seemed a little surprised at the specificity of the request.

"Hmm. I think he is off-line at present. Let me see if-"

"His rest and recuperation is sufficient-" said Mother.

"But R&R is designated for another two weeks…" stuttered Brunthe, before hesitating a little a little more at the silence. "Mother, you have access to all this information - I don't understand why you would pick someone - I mean, you are aware of his attitude - quite out of keeping for a Faith Seeker - almost maverick, really-" he said with some annoyance.

"Mandrake, I have decided, is the best person for this job. Send him to interrogate the captured Porc. But ensure he has another officer with him," said Mother with cool despatch.

"Very well-" said Brunthe, "someone to keep an eye on him… hmm. Ah, yes. I will send him in with FSO Constance." Immediately, Brunthe raised his hand and spoke in to his comms pack: "Brunthe here - new orders from Mother: deploy Mandrake!"

Mandrake marched through the corridors as fast as the ID scanners would allow - irritated at the way his pace was controlled by the technology. The corridors were nothing more than featureless tubes which glowed with the guidance colour - drone bays were amber. The glowing corridor irritated Mandrake - he disliked being inside a technology which controlled him - he always wanted to be on the outside, looking in. He always felt trapped on the inside; in fact, he thought to himself, he always felt trapped anyway. An alarm blared and a door jutting off the corridor flashed a signal: 'Drone Bay 437'. Aware of the slight flash of a retina detector, Mandrake impatiently waited for the door to open before entering the waiting area. Inside the small room, which continued in a featureless design, even down to the pull down resters, Mandrake surveyed the area. Entrance and exit, one screen, three resters, one camera, one drone pilot, one FSO.

"They are taking him to a cell", said the Faith Seeker sitting upright on a rester, looking intently at the viseo on the wall.

"It's too early - wait until we get there-" Mandrake ordered through his comms pack. He waited for a few moments, listening to the static inside his helmet before a reply was given.

"Message from Mother - there has been a delay," it stated in a grating voice. Mandrake was frustrated, and he took it out on the other FSO-

"What delay? Is this you?" Unable to see through the darkened face screen, he looked at her badge - 'FSO Constance' glowed in orange between the green laurel. Mandrake looked at her for a moment, summarily dismissed her from his consideration, then turned directly to the drone pilot who sat under the screen: "I'm ready to leave now - I don't need a backup!" he stated firmly, emphasising the words 'need' and 'now' as if he were speaking to an irritating child. The pilot glanced at Mandrake, about to explain that he was only following orders, but, sensing the tension between them, decided not to get involved in a dispute with two Faith Seekers.

"We always have a backup - that's the rule. It's nothing to do with me, Mandrake - I'm as ready and willing as you are!" said Constance. "Perhaps they want to try and get accurate information out of him before you get there and mangle it -" but she was instantly cut off:

"What do you mean - I'm one of the best decoders here," said Mandrake, raising his visor.

"You know what I mean - you studied biochology as

well as me - information extrapolated through severe biological disruption generates phantoms-" cutting her off again, he said:

"I know they'll say anything for the pain to stop - but they are not phantoms!"

"What they say is corrupted-" exclaimed Constance.

"Everything a Porc says is corrupted! You know that," replied Mandrake.

"Yes, I know - but they will say anything to stop the pain - we don't want *anything* - we want accurate information - we can't waste clean-up operations on inaccurate, well - we need to be sure, Mandrake!" Constance looked straight into his face - his eyes were focussed beyond her - he was like a hound that had spotted a hare - he was looking straight through her, his body statuesque in its stiffness, his pupils locked and narrowing. His consciousness had been re-focussed by the image now displayed on the viseo screen; spatial displacement triggered - his taught, sinuous-tensioned muscle structure fed through the exo-armour, his biological responses triggering as if he were in the cell at that moment. Aware that she was oblivious to him, Constance followed his gaze to see that the Porc survivor had been placed into the cell.

"His name's Deacon, apparently," said Constance, "not that it matters."

"It does matter. I care what his name is," said Mandrake softly. Constance looked a little surprised at what she took to be an irrelevance.

"You care about his name? He's just a Porc -"

"Yes, he is, but he has been given a name. A name suggests someone cares enough to give a name. A name means there is a path, a series of events where the name was arrived at. The name might be given by a parent, a carer, an institution - the name might be chosen by him or by those he serves. Whichever way, it has clues, meanings, pathways. It could be the way to trace him back to his nest," said Mandrake.

Constance was surprised by the application of analysis Mandrake had applied, by the logical and methodical sifting of information which may offer clues. He is very much in control of his emotions, she thought - he is a killing machine, as he and all Faith Seekers are bred to be, but she felt that somehow he was overstepping his role.

"They are all just Porcs - but they all carry clues. I can get the data out of him, I know I can," said Mandrake.

"The strategy we've been told to use is-" but Constance was interrupted.

"We have to apply a different strategy - I know a Porc will say anything when it's being hurt - they are human, of course, physiologically-" Mandrake stated.

"Conceded," stated Constance.

"And they will say whatever is wanted to make the pain stop - but, if you get enough data, from the same source, for a long period, through different methods..." he was becoming fervent, and Constance could see the blood lust glowing in his eyes - she thought she would allay it:

"Then you will have nothing but their bloody entrails spread all over the floor-" she said. Mandrake, still unmoving from the viseo screen, took off one of the armoured gloves so that he could emphasise with his bare hand.

"Yes - entrails, dripped in blood, fragments, but you

search through the bone and the flesh and the bile and you slip it all through your fingers, searching, feeling, and you'll find that some of those fragments of bone will fit together, you defragment and place in order-" He walked closer towards the viseo almost unconsciously –"you analyse the scent from the steaming flesh - enough to give a clue-" he raised his bare fingers to his nose and sniffed, before reaching out to Deacon's image - his face impassive, his eyes focus-locked on the screen.

Constance watched his pupils narrow and flicker jaggedly across the image on the screen, analysing every minute detail. His description of his methodology of Porc interrogation clearly showed his barely contained violence, which she felt was unprofessional and ineffective.

"You have some disgusting metaphors, Mandrake," she said. Mandrake didn't turn to her, but kept staring, fixated, at the face on the screen.

"What metaphors?" snarled Mandrake.

5

The Sisterhood of Tongues

Sunetra lifted her gaze skywards, following the majestic columns of trees, and closed her eyes against the beams of white light which streamed like arrows through the cooling canopy of green. She breathed in deeply, the air scented with damp woodland and pine. She swayed slightly as she started to undress, her FSO uniform unbuckling, unblocking, detaching from each section with a slight hiss which resembled a sigh. Sunetra's face rocked between the alternating strips of cool shadow, and the warm golden light of the sun. She looked down into the deep green reflection of the pool before her, and gazed at her image - with the top of her uniform removed she looked half human. The birds sang with a harmonious unity of purpose which seemed to cause her body to meld into the forest, she felt.

She stepped out of the bottom section of the uniform, and it stood still on its own, eerily resembling a dismembered torso, she thought. She peered for a moment, before stepping into the green woodland pool, it's deep stillness like a dark mirror. She glimpsed her reflection in the pool, the curved contours and sweep of hips - she half closed her eyes and then fractured the stillness with her hands - she did not want to see the dark angular slices which raged through the curve of her stomach - she did not want to see below her waist. She did not want to see what they had done. To every day feel her suffering was one thing, but to see it in her full-bodied reflection, her face attached, was sometimes too much to bear. The broken water started to catch the bright beams of light, and flashed in her eyes irritatingly, and as she closed them, her vision dissolved into another place...

Far away from Sunetra, in a cavern lit by tall candles, atop tall holders of gold and silver, flickered the image of a man, a man in torment but with a strange look on his face as though sentiency were lost to him. They would say he would seem to be 'at peace'. The man was not real, but was very carefully and intricately carved to show every dripping sore, every weeping wound across his back - a meticulous detail of the thorns imbedded in his head, the oozing blood clotting in globules at his side. And the angular, squared nub of the iron nails, oversized and forcefully penetrating his flesh - hammered through so hard they exited through the wood of the cross. The whole cavernous chamber reverberated to the sound of a knell, eerily determined in its persistence. Prostrated on the floor, in front of this huge idol, was a woman. She was draped in robes of black and white, covered from the top of her head to the soles of her feet. A cowl hiding her face, she stood up and turned to face the chanting crowd. All identical to her - the black and white throng undulated at her words.

"Sisters, I have been given a message. Two of our brothers have been saved. They have been protected from death - but they are in the evil hands of the Faith Seekers..." at which mention the gathering hissed vociferously.

"And so we have been given a task - a task to prove our devotion," continued the sister. The knell became louder, louder, as the multitudinous bodies of the sisters swayed back and forth. Throwing her arms in the air in supplication signalled the start of a movement from above - the sound of huge wooden gears, clockwork-like, ratchets turning jaggedly as the sister cried out:

"Behold! Let the sins of Mother be visited upon her children!" A huge wooden cage containing captured Faith Seekers started its descent into the crowd, and the knell turned from a solemn, stately pace to the rising beat of a war drum, clanging furiously.

At the sight of the caged enemies descending the congregation of Sisters parted their habits feverishly, and bared the glimmer of knives concealed in their robes - knives of many shapes and sizes. The sight of the descent was too wonderful to behold, and the Sisters bristled with silver blades as they were transmogrified, crying out in an ecstasy of tongues.

Sunetra's eyes rolled at the flashing in her eyes, and she started to lose her balance, placing her hands in the water, where another hand griped it. Steadying herself, she opened her eyes and looked into the pool to see the kind hand which had helped her - and it was the dismembered hand of a child. Confused, she recoiled, again losing her balance as the sight of the water which had been turned to blood, with floating body parts bobbing up and down all around her. She tried to wade her way out of the pool, but her strength was weakened against the   fast clotting of the blood pool, and she felt herself being dragged under. Desperately breathing hard with the exertion, her nostrils flared at the smell of the iron in the blood as they clogged under the congealing water…

Sunetra suddenly found a new wave of energy as she was startled awake by the sound of a jarring alarm - her eyes suddenly opening wide. Running out of the pool she grabbed her comms pack and answered:

"Yes, Mother. I am rested now. I am tranquil and ready to interrogate the Porc. Ready him for my arrival." Looking back, she could see nothing of the nightmare she had just been in. It was all an hallucination. Sunetra called out:

"Computer - return to normal mode" she ordered whereupon the vision of the woodland glade and lake dissolved back into the bare white walls and tiles of the recuperation room. All evidence of the hallucination was gone from the room, and Sunetra pulled on a clean white t-shirt, but the angular slices which darkly ruptured the gentle white of her tight t-shirt was the real evidence - covered over, but always present. Sunetra took a deep breath and readied herself to interrogate the Porc.

6

The Cell

A beam of light shot down from the heavens and awoke Deacon with a start - unable to shield his eyes with his wrists held in chains, he turned his head away as he realized the light he was bathed in was not the sign of hope, but the signal for interrogation. He slowed down his breathing, and began to have an awareness of his surroundings - he knew he had to buy himself time before the interrogation started. He had been given food and drink, and then lay down, and must have fallen asleep, he thought to himself. He opened his eyes again - the light was bright, but it was only in his face because he had looked in its direction. It was the sun - it was a lovely sunny day and he was sitting in a meadow, with the sun on his face and birds singing around him. The food! He was so tired after the food. They'd tranquillised him, he was drugged, surely, but then he thought no - they would simply have injected him if they'd wanted to. They had complete control over him. No, the tiredness was his body responding to the enormous stress it had just been through. Seeing the hundreds of his brethren killed around him: it had all been planned so well - how were they betrayed? Who was it? Deacon went through all the scenarios of betrayal, espionage, revenge - he refused to entertain the thought that no one had been responsible for the finding of the priest hole except Mother. Someone would have to pay. There were probably many involved, thought Deacon. There might have to be a spectacle made of them - something to ensure others would not follow in their steps towards betrayal.

Why only him? He fully expected to die - he had been caught before, as a teenager - caught, sent to faith school, and renounced all belief. But he soon secretly reverted - back into the arms of God - no matter how much they tried to decrypt him, as they called it. Once you have found God, he does not leave you - he always walks at your side. You might have to hide it from the infidels, but he knew how to do that. He was very good at that. Sunday school had taught him well. All around him the machine guns blazed. Yet God had given him the control to think, to plan, and to sacrifice the brethren needed for his survival - they would be in heaven, anyway, so it was no loss. He was needed here on Earth. His time would come when God chose - and he had much work to do before that time came. He had been picked out from the crowd. Saved. It must surely be a sign, he thought. Yes of course - a sign! He had been spared to bear witness! He had been chosen! He had chosen him. To spread the word - that you can be saved! That he is watching over you - that there is a plan.

Deacon's thoughts ran on and on, until he suddenly

realised that the birds had stopped singing, that he was no longer in a meadow, but sat on a chair in a plain white room and was startled to see a woman in white standing in front of him - he was jolted by the surge of adrenalin which rushed through him:

"I'm Takako. I'm a teacher here at the Faith School." A woman of Japanese descent, in her 30s, her simple plain white clothes were topped by the jet-black hair which framed her face. The only mark on her white uniform was the laurel wreath - the same green emblem emblazoned but with 'Teacher' written underneath. Deacon said nothing for a moment, assessing the situation he now found himself in. Takako spoke again:

"I gave the order for you to be fed, and rested, and now you are feeling better, I want to talk to you," she said gently. Deacon's awareness of his surroundings expanded to bring an ominous figure in black into his field of view - he immediately tried to launch himself forward, but felt his arms and wrists yanked back by the solidity of the chains. "I have a Faith Seeker here with me - just so we are not alone-" Takako was interrupted by Deacon shouting:

"You gave the order for my people to be slaughtered!" he roared. Sunetra gave no response, but stood immovable, emotionless and taut. Takako interrupted his outburst:

"The Faith Seeker was only carrying out orders. All those people were convicted criminals - people of religious conviction. And we know what happens to people convicted of practicing religion. Now, let's move forward, shall we? Now I've been told a little bit about you -" but Deacon was not listening - he was putting his mind back to the task of escape.

"Faith Seeker Officer Sunetra is right in what she said - she said I have to watch you," but there was no response from Deacon. "I know what you're doing," said Takako wearily. He glanced at her - did she know, he thought?

"I am a man defending my faith, appointed by God!" said Deacon with steely conviction.

"You're checking me, the cell, and your surroundings for weaknesses - for clues - what tech does it have - is there a chink in the amour? Well - the armour is there!" She pointed at Sunetra, "And she tells me you've been trained - well trained. She says you were dressed as a priest, but you fought as a soldier. That combination indicates that you are a terrorist - someone who has been trained to murder and torture innocent people who do not believe in the same things as you. You have nothing to say?" Takako waited for a moment, looking over her shoulder towards Sunetra, as if she were about to order her to participate in the questioning. It was enough to encourage a response.

"You are murderers. You massacre in cold blood, my flock and their families - our brethren, brothers and sisters - everyone who is loved and dear to me - do you think you can then talk with me? You have nothing in you but hatred and vile corruption!" Deacon spat across at her, defiantly, and then waited for the expectant blows. None come - Takako looked down at her uniform, and with a sigh, reached in to her pocket and took out some tissue. She carefully wiped the spit from her face and clothes, glanced over towards Sunetra and shook her head to indicate that she should lower her gun - Deacon was not even aware that the Faith Seeker had raised it. Takako walked over and dropped the tissue into an incinerator which instantly disintegrated the tissue. She walked back over and stood firmly in front of Deacon, and spoke with control and clarity in her voice:

"This is a school - a place of learning. The first lesson to learn is that it is not your god who has let you live - it is Mother." Deacon thought how ironic it was that she should say that - he knew that God had saved him. He could only smile at the woman's self-deception.

"You have been brought to Faith School - you are to be given a second chance. But before that can happen you must learn and understand two things," Takako informed him. "Mother has the power over your life and death,' she continued. "It is Mother that you look to for life. It is Mother that you look to for death. Learn that first lesson." Takako stood firmly before him, her authority and power clear. "The jail you are in is of your own making. The prison which holds you are your beliefs. Mother can give you your freedom. Just repent of all your religious beliefs. Repent and be saved. Freedom is achieved once belief is destroyed. Do not believe in a god - believe in Mother!"

Back at the Mother Board, the echoing chamber was only lit now by the warm glow of Mother; towering above Brunthe, busily at work on a screen at the laurel dais, he arched his neck giddily upwards in response to a change in colour: her hologram was changing from a warm smile of comfort to an expression of anguish:

"They are on the move, Brunthe - they are attempting to locate him," she said with solemnity.

"So quickly!" said Brunthe. "Where do they get this information from? How do they-"

"They are moving, looking, seeking him out. I think

this is confirmation enough that he is someone of significance. I think I am right in my belief - he is a trailblazer," said Mother.

"Ah, yes, a trailblazer, as you thought..." said Brunthe with satisfaction, "and likely to light a trail all the way to their den."

"Our priority is to ensure the safety of the Faith School, of course," said Mother.

"I'll withdraw some drone squadrons and send them," said Brunthe matter-of-factly.

"No," Mother replied simply.

"Mother?" questioned Brunthe.

"The movement might draw attention. The drones' flight to their defence might be what the Porcs are looking for - we don't want to lead them straight to the school," said Mother, and waited for his response.

"Of course not, Mother. Their intelligence can be very good... very, rapid," he said, choosing the word carefully.

"I prefer 'cunning' to 'intelligence'," said Mother, "Let's wait for them to make their move, search for how they gathered that information, then outrun them."

"Of course, Mother. I will ready the drones and squadrons, but with strict instructions for secrecy, of course," Brunthe said with an air of resignation.

"I will never give up my faith - I will die first!" said Deacon with fierce defiance.

"Well, that's not much of a sacrifice - after all - he'll go straight to heaven and save himself a lot of pain - he's got nothing to lose! No sacrifice at all... it's just what he wants. I don't understand why those Porcs don't just immediately kill themselves and save us all a great deal of trouble," said drone pilot Chetino. He looked away from the viseo screen to the two Faith Seekers he was sharing the cell with. There was no response. He remembered what they were and though he would be better off asking a direct question - "What do you think?" he said to the female FSO.

"Mother wants two questions answered: 'How have you been able to avoid us for so long, and where is the location of your nerve centre'," stated Constance. Chetino felt uneasy alone in the room with these two FSOs. They were transfixed on the interrogation, and with all that adrenaline coursing through their veins it felt very edgy to try and while away the time.

"I want to know everything that's going on in that cell!" said Mandrake, still transfixed on the screen. "Zoom in on the Porc's face," he ordered, and the screen flared and filled with Deacon's face.

"We need to be there - I don't understand the delay," said Constance.

"Focus on his face - everything that is going on in that cell that I need to know is in his face. I have seen it before - I am sure," said Mandrake.

"Where - can you remember?" asked Constance.

"There have been so many faces. I don't know. I want to see what's going on in those dark, dark eyes of his," said Mandrake.

"Off with your metaphors again," said drone pilot Chetino.

"I've already told you - I don't use metaphors," whispered Mandrake, as he stared intently at the screen.

"Dark, dark eyes," said Chetino. "His eyes are bright, shining with Porc-light," he said.

"Religious conviction. Seeing right through reality, as

if this world was a ghost," explained Mandrake. Chetino was about to mention the word 'metaphor' again, but thought the better of it. He was suddenly aware of Mandrake looking straight into his face, his breath heavy.

"What is your problem, Mandrake?" he said, becoming irritated himself - trapped in the cell, waiting for the drone, he suddenly felt unnerved - the Faith Seeker's levels of anxiety exhibited uncontrolled behaviour.

"I don't understand what the delay is - why, if they have Sunetra doing the interrogation, do they need to send me?" said Mandrake.

"Us. They are sending us," said Constance.

"Mother! Answer me!" Mandrake asked, but only static came back over the speaker.

Back in the cell, Takako continued to question Deacon:

"Look Deacon - you have been given a second chance - the Faith Seeker here-" she nodded towards Sunetra- "she found it very hard not to kill you - but that is not what we do here. The Faith School is about giving you all a second chance - you will be tagged and allowed your freedom again - but only once you have cooperated and repented," continued Takako. Deacon looked around and thought of an idea - he suddenly became energised, and said:

"I refuse to talk anymore until I have had my request granted," he said firmly. Takako raised her eyebrows in surprise.

"And what is this request?" she asked.

"I wish to see my child," he said plainly.

7

The Faith School

Deacon was not surprised that they had complied with his request to see his child - it was one of the many tricks he had at his disposal; it was a procedure which worked well - to use their own laws to work to your advantage, to protect you when you intended them harm, to exploit their vulnerabilities is a time-honoured tactic. He knew that they would soon enough identify that he was not the father of the child, but in the time it bought, he would be given many opportunities. The Faith Seeker escorting him was unresponsive to any questions - she just kept walking him through the school, corridor after corridor, class after class. Deacon knew he had very little chance of escape - but he was watching - the structure, the materials, the possible escape routes - watching every little detail - who knew what would be relevant until the time came? Any weakness - no matter how small, can be magnified - for a moment these words took him back to his priest training: 'Look for any weakness, even their mightiest monuments, with one small crack, can be wedged' they said, 'and with the constant drip of doubt, any lack of faith will spread and multiply, until the solid ground they walk on starts to tremble and their monuments - their scientific beliefs - will tumble down around them'. Deacon felt satisfied when he remembered this.

Passing through the pupils of the Faith School, Deacon scanned as many faces as possible - he recognised many of them - and many recognised him - the adults knew not to acknowledge him, but they children - they could be a problem. His mind was still racing for clues, sifting through information, trying to find something of significance. Still walking, exchanging looks with different children, Deacon suddenly clicked on to the game. Mother was, of course, watching. On the viseo screens, she monitored all the reactions as he was moved through room after room. Mother was watching for any signs of recognition - Deacon talked loudly, eager for Mother and all those monitoring to know he was aware of their plans:

"Is this tour for my benefit? Or is it an identity parade?" Deacon called, smiling broadly at all those around him. Watching on the screen, Mother gave orders to the escorts:

"Keep him there, Sunetra. Watch him carefully - he seems quite at home there - as if he's in familiar territory," said Mother to Brunthe, who replied:

"Yes - he seems quite plucky. I don't like it when they're not afraid," he said. "Keep him there, Sunetra," said Brunthe over the comms channel.

"Stop!" said Sunetra as she yanked on his arms, causing him to wince. They stopped near a large panoramic window with views of the valley below. He could see a meandering river of green, a crystal clear blue sky with just cotton-wool puffs of cloud - he couldn't recognise the scene below - it was a beautiful view, an idyllic view in fact - an absolute Garden of Eden, he thought. But it didn't seem to match up with the information he'd worked out from his transport here - the sun was rising on the wrong side - can this be right, he thought? Sending the coordinates here would be disastrous if they were wrong. Deacon pretended to stumble, falling against the class window - the whole valley down below bulged and distorted under the pressure. Deacon stared incredulously.

"There are no real windows here, Deacon - that would be a security risk - these are all vizeoblinds." Takako stood opposite him, and motioned for Sunetra to allow him to sit down.

"Look around you - what do you see?" she asked. Deacon used the invitation to paint more detail onto his image of the school: it was a scene of playfulness, of light and happiness. The interior was circular, with gardens, ponds, playgrounds, a menagerie and playing fields. The majority there were children, though ranging up through teenagers and even to young adults. Some children ran noisily, others, in the secluded zones, read books, or had stories read to them. Deacon looked upwards - a beautiful summer's day, with the whitest small puffs of clouds on a picture-perfect deep blue sky, the sun full and warm, unobscured. Deacon looked directly at the sun - it did not burn his eyes - it was bright, but clearly not the sun. He turned back to face Takako, and aimed his words at her and Sunetra, making them loud for Mother to clearly hear, too.

"I see a fantasy. A fiction created by Mother. A

prison where all traces of humanity are removed from these poor, unfortunate captives. Hand them back to God - and give them their freedom!" said Deacon contemptuously.

"This is a school. A school is a place of learning. I hope you will learn something," said Takako.

"I have learnt much already. I have learnt that you create prisons that you call schools, indoctrinate instead of educate, crush instead of grow-" Sunetra was ordered to cut his speech short:

"Do you not want to see your son? To know that he is safe?" she asked. She looked closely at Deacon's face, and, with the momentary confusion displayed, she could see that he had forgotten about this original request. Looking around at the groups playing, Deacon saw a child, with similar blond hair, fair complexion and - yes, he knew him, he was sure. He shouted out:

"Son! Come to me." The boy looked around, and stared towards him with recognition, which, for a moment, made Takako think that she had been given incorrect information by Sunetra - that she was mistaken in her belief that he was not Deacon's son.

"That's my father's coat!" He said, and Takako was reassured. Deacon replied directly to the boy:

"Yes - it is. He asked me to take it. So you would know him through me. Do you remember me?" asked Deacon.

"Yes - yesterday-" stumbled the boy.

"That's right - I did everything I could to try and save your family, I-"

"I remember you," called another voice. Deacon turned to the voice, and it was that of a child older than this one, a teenager, also blond and fair.

47

"Do you indeed? Now, let me look at you, hmm. Yes - now I remember you," Deacon said slowly, his eyes inviting the boy to make his name known.

"My name is Jude… I-" the boy stammered, eager to know this man, eager to ask him something.

"Ah, yes, Jude. The boy Jude," said Deacon, before turning abruptly away and back to the boy he had tried to pass off as his son. "Now - your mother and father knew me, too - that's why they came to me last night - for protection-"

"But they're-" Deacon did not allow him to finish, quickly carrying on the story for him.

"I heard your mother's call for help, and I answered it - 'my child is not tagged' she said - and I saved you - I showed you the secret tunnel to escape, I tried to save you all. Do you not remember?" asked Deacon emphatically.

"Yes. I remember," said the boy, who unconsciously reached out to touch his father's coat. Immediately his arm was clenched in Sunetra's iron fist- "For your safety, Joshua - to keep you safe," said Takako. Deacon smiled at the boy.

"Joshua. My name is Deacon, and I will not harm you - you are my child-" he started, warmly, before suddenly seeing the boy became angry, flashing hatred in his eyes:

"I'm not your child - I have - I have a father," said the boy with tears welling in his eyes.

"I know you do," responded Deacon, satisfied by how quickly he was cut off at the word 'child' - Joshua wanted him to know who his father was. Deacon was perceptive - and saw another small crack to rend, another weakness to work upon; he whispered quickly:

"And he gave me a message to pass on to you," before suddenly turning back to the boy Jude.

"And you, Jude. Do you know where your mother is?" he asked bluntly.

"No," said Jude, after a long pause, and looked nervously around the room, like an animal looking for s way out.

"No?" Deacon gave the word that blended tone that synthesised incredulity, curiosity and puzzlement. He looked intently at Jude because he already knew the answer - he just wanted the little boy to say it. Aloud. To him. It would be his first intimate touch. A probe. He'll just wait for it to push a little deeper before he exerts some more pressure to jab in.

"But we all have a mother. Don't we?" Deacon asked.

"My mother is gone," said the boy, his head slightly bowed, his eyes averted from Deacon with a shame which came from he knew not where.

"Ah. Gone." Deacon clasped both his hands together loosely, brought them up to his chin and lent his head forward and a little to the side. He lowered his voice and said gently, "I don't believe that a mother would leave such a lovely boy as you. A mother loves her child with all her heart, and would never leave her son alone. I've never known a mother to do that. She would fight and fight. She must have been taken. Taken away from you." Deacon could just make out the little sheen of moisture beginning to shine over the boy's eyes, before he spoke furiously:

"She did fight! She did! And now she's dead. She did! She did! And now she's dead," said Jude, once to the interlocutor, and once more in confirmation to himself. A deep breath welled from him and his face contorted. Out of nowhere the intimate moment was snatched away by Sunetra's black-gloved hands snapping Deacon's arms back and lifting him away from the boy. Takako stood in the doorway and called to the boy with a raised arm.

"Come to me, Jude. We don't want you upset. You have been making such good progress," she said, with a warm tone to her voice but with a cold look towards the restrained man. "Both of you come to me," and signalled to the Faith Seeker to take Deacon away. Sunetra gripped Deacon in a vice-like grip, and dragged him away as he shouted out fiercely:

"She's not dead, Jude! *She is not dead!* I know where she is - I can lead you to her!" His tone was one of utter conviction, and of such certainty that it penetrated deeply. He had to help the boy understand, he thought. Deacon shouted desperately as he was pulled further away. The boy Jude twisted his head as Takako led him away and looked straight into Deacons' eyes - they seemed to connect and burn straight into him. Deacon's lips curled into the slightest smile, for he knew now that his Parthenon shot would penetrate deeply - he shouted again:

"She's not dead, Jude! She is not dead. I know where she is - I can lead you to her!"

"If you wish to leave this cell alive, then you must cooperate," said Sunetra, without looking at him. Deacon was back in the cell, restrained and angry, his leg was bouncing on the ball of his foot. "Mother is losing patience with you. You lied about your son, you used the opportunity to try and recce the school and you tried to infiltrate children's minds who are in the middle of processing. You are of no value, I would have destroyed you immediately," said Sunetra flatly. She awaited Deacon's response - he sat brooding for several minutes before answering.

"I must be of value -even Mother knows that - or she would have allowed you to kill me in the street market," he said. "Of no value? No - you are the one of no value. A cloned killer dropped off the end of a conveyer belt..." Deacon replied.

"A captured Porc would normally be assigned a teacher. But there is something different about you - it is very unusual for a Porc to survive to such an age without tagging," said Sunetra. "How did you survive for so long? You must be nearly thirty," she asked.

"Oh, I didn't do it alone. I couldn't possibly have done it alone, as you know. Deep in your heart, you know I could not have done it alone," said Deacon with some certainty.

"Who helped you? Who was it?" said Sunetra methodically. There was a pause. Deacon looked down, down to the floor, then breathed through his nose, closed his lips tightly and thought carefully. He looked up, then down, seemingly wrestling with his conscience. He looked straight at her.

"If I tell you-"

"Yes?" interrupted Sunetra hungrily.

"They will be very angry that I have betrayed them - I will pay the consequences-" he said, before Sunetra encouraged him:

"You will be protected - there is nothing for you to fear, Deacon - no one can harm you hear. No one can reach you," she reassured him. "This is a place of ... sanctuary. You can talk here. Who helped you evade detection for so long? Who is supporting you?" Deacon looked anxiously back and forth, unsure of which way to go.

"There is no point - he will reach me. You cannot protect me!" announced Deacon.

"No -one can reach you - you are safe - who is it?" Sunetra demanded.

"You won't believe me - it will be for nothing! If I betray my supporter - it, it won't stop you doing what, what you're going to do to me - because - you will not believe me," he said with an air of hopelessness in his voice, an expression of futile despair wrought upon his face.

"Who is it?" she coaxed. Deacon looked straight and deep into her eyes. Deacon's hands, bound behind him, clenched and opened in mimicry of his mind, before opening, relaxed - and as they relaxed so did his face clear from the confusion, and he looked up at Sunetra, returning her gaze.

"The Lord God. He has stood at my side these many years past... protector of my soul!" His voice starting to tremble with passion and rise and rise with a certainty only achieved through blinkered and unswerving conviction. Deacon continued:

"What do you know of souls? You do not have one! You are just a clone, a factory girl, a chick allowed to grow for a little while before fulfilling her created purpose - to be eaten by the war machine Mother! You could never even hope to understand!" Deacon continued, his intonation rising in pitch with each assertion. Sunetra turned her back and glanced at the viseo camera watching them, immediately concealing the look of disinterest on her face - so many times had she been through this, so many times. Now the routine should start - now she would start to show her superior skills as a Faith Seeker. She looked down at her black gauntlet, studded with chrome, and clenched it into a wrecking ball...

The viseo from the cell transmitted this scene to the Mother Board, and Brunthe commented:

"Yes, Mother - I do see a slight reduction in her ability to control her, mmm, spirit, shall we say?" Mother was less subtle -

"Sunetra's behaviour is bordering on the side of emotional. I think the time has come for her retirement, Brunthe - it comes to us all," said Mother.

"She has been a superb officer, Mother - and given many years of-" but Brunthe was overridden by Mother:

"Instruct her to withdraw from the interrogation - she can still be very useful to us, Brunthe," Mother ordered.

Sunetra's fist unclenched as she heard the cell door unlock, and she walked towards it, ignoring the ranting Deacon, who was straining against his chains to try and raise himself up and praise the wonders of his god.

"Seekers - restrain and sedate," ordered Sunetra as she passed through the door, at which command two FSOs marched in and pushed on his shoulders to force him back down into his chair. As one flicked a small canister under his nose and hissed a gas into his nostrils which flared with anger, the other fired a Taser at his temple which caused him to immediately drop motionless and slumped, held upright only by his taut bonds.

As Sunetra walked through the corridor a viseodrone followed her, projecting a hologram of Mother in front of her as she walked.

"Yes, Mother?" Sunetra asked.

"I have relieved you from this interrogation - I have assigned this Porc to someone else. Please go and ready yourself - I have another mission for you. I need your talents elsewhere," said Mother warmly.

"Yes, Mother. I will prepare immediately," Sunetra replied.

"There is little time - you will have nutrition and rest aboard the drone - it will fly through the night. Please install your uniform and board the drone awaiting you in Section 9," said Mother.

Sunetra walked fast towards her rest room - to be given another mission half way through an interrogation indicated some urgency elsewhere, thought Sunetra, though she wondered why it had never happened before. It was late in the Faith School, and the lighting was in night mode. A feint and comforting amber light pervaded the building. Sunetra walked past the sign to the children's sleeping quarters and hesitated. Something in the placement of the words 'children' and 'sleeping' made her want to act compulsively. She did not understand these hesitancies in her behaviour anymore - they were becoming uncontrollable. And these words made an image in her mind which caused her to act compulsively. She never got to see children sleeping unless it was on a raid, and more often than not, she then had to kill them. There was something pleasant in seeing them sleeping peacefully without having to make an intervention.

'She is not dead.' Those four words ricocheted around Jude's mind. All night his body flipped back and forth, one side to the other, jolting and jigging in his bed as the invisible chains from his mind pulled one way, then the other in a macabre puppet show - as those words ricocheted back and forth, so his body tossed and turned. As the sun rose at the dawn of a new day, Jude's face was paled and his eyes were dulled and darkened by the restlessness of his spirit. Some bullets were magical. And this bullet: 'She is not dead', seemed to be magical in that it would never lose the power to ricochet endlessly around his mind. A biological drive for the love of his mother had been cruelly turned into a metaphysical quest beyond the realms of reality. Jude's mother was dead. But she had been resurrected by Deacon. In one brief meeting, an innocent had been manipulated and abused in the most calculating and purposeful manner - one where Deacon would assume the guise of a helper, a friend and a saviour, and where a loving and caring mother had been dug out of the grave and paraded like some grotesque Frankenstein to be the marionette to make a child dance for his pleasure. Deacon knew that if you found an animal's weakness it made it all the easier to set a snare - a snare that pulls tighter and tighter as you wrestle in a desperate bid to escape. A snare that loosens and lets you breathe, and takes away some of the pain if you stop fighting, and accept that you are captured. The word is mighty indeed. Through Deacon's words have come the power of life over death - Jude's mother has been resurrected in the mind of her child. She is not dead.

8

Lessons at Gunpoint

Jude was so tired that even the amber night light hurt his eyes - eyes which felt heavy, lids fused together, his body aching and his mind slow. So tired. The warm, forgiving softness of the pillow conjured up the cocoon-like feel he used to have with his mother - nestled into her, safe. He looked through the lash bars of his sticky lids and, bathed in the amber light he could see that where there should be no one was someone: there was a ghost in the chair; it was watching him. The shape was feminine, but dark and spectral. But it was definitely a woman. It was his mother. Watching him asleep as she used to when he was ill. Never leaving his side. Safe. It was true - she was not dead. He suddenly became aware of another body in his bed - his toes touching it like an unknown beast in the deep sea. His eyes widened into sharp focus and he jumped and called out in terror. He was then joined by another scream - at the foot of the bed emerged the unknown body - and it too screamed in terror at the watcher in the chair. The dark spectral figure moved with an unnatural speed and seemed to summon out of thin air a weapon which whined as it charged in readiness to fire.

Deacon prayed hard. He prayed hard because he needed to exude as much energy as possible - it was a long way for prayers to travel, but he knew it could be done - he had done it many times before. He joined his hands in a triangulated formation, and upon those hands were tattoos - blue bones sketched out, indicating the mortality and final form of the body within. As he touched the two tips together and then completed the triangulation with his bowed face, he felt a tingle - a sensation that started to draw energy from within. He knew that help would be on its way as soon as they were able. His Sisters would not leave him here. They knew that he had been captured. He threw his head back and his hands to his shoulders - palms upright in an ecstatic pose for the camera. He used the opportunity to glance at it - it was there alright, watching. Constantly watching - that was why he must continue to put on a good show for them. He had an audience. And he knew it.

He breathed deep. He rolled his eyes upwards in a feverish embrace with an invisible force. His mouth opened into a dark cavern and burped strange sounds.

"Extraordinary," muttered Brunthe to himself, losing interest immediately and busying himself with work.

"Brunthe, you should be paying attention," chided Mother.

"I have much work to do," replied Brunthe with an air of having seen it all many times before - an ennui which was genuine and ran very deep inside him.

"But you know how Porc leaders work - if they are doing something dramatic it is because they are like magicians. They are magicians are they not?" asked Mother.

"Yes, I know," said Brunthe absently, "If he is doing anything overly dramatic it is merely a slight of hand to distract from the trick. He is clearly trying to stop you seeing what he is really doing while he 'communes' or 'prays' or whatever term he uses. Oh, yes - I am well aware, Mother. But I am also well aware that you have foreseen all of this. I trust you entirely, Mother, so that I may be able to get on with the other business." Brunthe smiled at Mother, and was about to walk away to continue his work when Mother became alarmed. Her image glowed with a slight amber of warning.

"The video signal is being intercepted - they are breaking through. I'm trying to trace the breach. Ready the Faith Seekers - sound the alarms," said Mother with some urgency, giving instructions to herself, rather like the Oracle at Delphi who, in her glimmering face, could be seen an otherworldliness of connection.

Mother is looking at the video being relayed from Deacon's cell. He is on his knees, bent over his bed, with his hands clasped together. Praying, praying. Brunthe, peering above his glasses at the scene in the cell, wondered aloud - "and will his prayers be answered, Mother?" he asked.

"I think that this time they will. I am waiting for a response. We have drones positioned around the faith school.

"Please don't don't kill me! Please!" screamed Jude, forced to close his eyes from the flashing of the red laser sight in his eyes. As Sunetra moved the gun rapidly back and forth between each boy's head, the other cried out, whimpering, unable to catch his breath, his eyes starting to roll upwards till the whites filled the sockets.

"Please - we're frightened!" said Jude, choking with fear. The figure lowered the gun, seeing the smaller boy was losing consciousness, and stood up - as her face entered the amber light Jude could see it was the female Faith Seeker. She leaned over the smaller boy and checked his pulse.

"He's hyperventilating," she said - "he needs to control his breathing," but gave no move to help him. Jude moved carefully, slowly, keeping his hands by his head and his eyes on Sunetra. She stayed motionless, and he slid himself to the bottom of the bed before putting an arm around the smaller boy, stroking his hair, and gently talking him round.

"It's OK, Josh - it's fine - she's not going to hurt us - it's fine," he said, gently rocking the bed. The smaller boy started to breathe slower, and to regain consciousness - as his eyes opened, they widened at the sight of Sunetra standing stolidly over him:

"I'm frightened," he managed to whisper to Jude, who then looked to Sunetra pleadingly.

"Could you sit down, please? Standing over him like that - it, it's scary - he's frightened," said Jude. Sunetra looked at each in turn, and then she knelt down at the side of the bed, and, with her head level with theirs, said:

"I won't hurt you -I'm frightened too."

A stalemate had been reached in the bedroom - the two children sat huddled together for protection, and Sunetra sat opposite; there was silence as each went through their thoughts. Josh stared mutely at the killer of his family, Jude stared because he could not understand why she was there - in his experience, if a Faith Seeker came to you in the middle of the night, it was for one reason only - to end your life.

"How can you be frightened?" asked Jude, "Why are you here?"

"I don't know why I'm frightened," said Sunetra simply, "and I'm here to protect you. But I should not be here."

"It' s alright - I shouldn't be here either. I came to see Josh. I wanted to talk to him, you see," said Jude, though he was struggling to find the words to explain what he wanted to talk to him about. "It's alright. There's nothing to worry about," said Jude to Josh who was struggling to understand. Jude tried to make sense of things. It was not his mother, he knew that now, of course. He had been dreaming.

"I sat here because you were crying. You were frightened," said Sunetra.

"But it was you who frightened me - I thought you were a ghost! I thought you were my-" he tailed off. Did she not understand that it was she who had frightened him?

"No - I was walking past and you were crying. I think you were having a bad dream," said Sunetra. "You were talking about your mother. Do you think about your mother every day?" she asked.

"Yes," he replied. Sunetra's face remained blank. There was silence for several minutes against the background of the quiet sobbing of Josh. Jude thought of something.

"And what about you? Do you think about your

mother every day?" he asked.

"Of course, I think about her all the time. I talk to her all the time," said Sunetra with a note of incomprehension in her voice.

"I see - so - do you live with her?" he continued.

"Live with her? Yes. Mother is everywhere. But she is not here now. In this room." Jude realised what the Faith Seeker was saying now.

"I understand what you are saying - but I don't mean *the* Mother - I mean *your* mother. The one who made you - gave birth to you. You know, your mother." Sunetra showed a slight puzzlement again.

"Mother is my mother. Mother made me. Mother did give birth to me. She is my mother," recited Sunetra.

"That's right!" said another voice at the door. "Mother is your mother." It was the teacher - she already had her hands in the air, knowing that Sunetra would immediately target her. In a whirl, Sunetra was in combat position, the red laser guidance playing around the teacher's forehead. She lowered her gun, and stood up.

"And I don't think Mother has given you permission to come here, FSO Sunetra. And the same goes for you, Jude. I would like to know - what is going on, please?" asked the teacher. Sunetra stood immobile, facing her, and Jude thought for a moment that he would cover for her.

"I was having a nightmare - I came to see Josh because I was frightened. Sunetra heard us crying, and came in to check that we were OK," he said, rather satisfied with his explanation. "And I was just asking about her mother," he added, trying to remember all the bits he had to cover to make the story plausible.

"I see. Thank you, FSO Sunetra. That was... kind of you," said the teacher with a bafflement she found hard to contain. "You must have been a great comfort to them." Even Jude could pick up on the sardonic tone of this last statement.

"This must be a new experience for the officer - Faith Seekers, you see, are clones. They don't have a real mother, like you and I," she said, oblivious to the insensitivity of her tense regarding the two boys. Jude suddenly felt the need to defend her again:

"I don't think that's very nice!" he blurted out. There was quiet in the room until the teacher replied, measuring her words:

"You don't think what is very nice, Jude?"

"Well... that you say things like that in front of her face - that she doesn't have a mother... that she-" but Jude was quickly cut off by the teacher-

"But she doesn't, Jude. She doesn't have a mother, she doesn't have feelings, she doesn't care. She is not human - she is a killing machine designed and built by Mother to kill Porcs - you should know that," said the teacher with a cruel twist- "this is one of the lessons you are here to learn, Jude. What is real and what is not - you are putting human feelings onto objects which are not human - can you remember what I taught you – what this is called?" she asked, raising her intonation in expectation of the correct answer.

"Personification," said Jude. "I'm sorry - I'm just personifying her - she does not have feelings, I understand that now - thank you for explaining to me," he rolled out flatly. The teacher was very pleased.

"Very well. Good. Now, let's all ready ourselves for

the day's teaching ahead," she said, addressing the two boys. She then turned to Sunetra - "Thank you, FSO Sunetra - please return to your duties." Sunetra did not answer, but walked immediately out of the room. As the teacher left, Jude was still left with a nagging thought in his head, a doubt about something the teacher had said - if it is true about Faith Seekers - then why did that one come in to comfort them, and say the things she did?

9

Revealing the Witch

"Mother's sealed the doors - looks like we're here till she's ready," said Mandrake, still trying to open the seal anyway.

"I don't think we should try and interfere with that - Mother obviously has a reason to keep us waiting," said the drone pilot. "What's the point - Mother will only sanction you if you break it," he continued. Mandrake turned towards the pilot, raising his visor and looking down at him - the pilot was suddenly cowed by the look − a wave of terror swept through him−

"I mean − we don't want to end up in trouble…" he faltered, hoping that he was defusing the situation. With no response, he looked at the Faith Seeker's badge - under the laurel and gold emblem was the name 'Mandrake'. "I'm not trying to give you, orders, Mandrake - I'm not telling you what to do," he pleaded. Mandrake turned back to trying to open the seal on the door.

"I like to find out how these things work - you never

know when you might need to break out..." he said.

"It's our own tech! You'll never need that - you want to find out how to infiltrate Porc tech," the drone pilot was aware that everything he said was antagonizing this Faith Seeker. The other one – the female, FSO Constance, seemed placid enough, but this one was really on edge, thought the pilot. 'Mandrake', he thought to himself, 'now where have I heard that name before?' He sat forward on the bench - you had to look hard at a Faith Seeker to try and figure them out - the uniform, a light-absorbing black - no reflections, no shining, no gloss - it was rather like staring into the eye of a shark - you know somewhere in that depth of darkness there was an intelligence - watching and calculating and planning. She looked the same, he thought - she was the same. He looked across at her she had closed her eyes and seemed to be resting - he took the opportunity to look carefully at her - staring at the face which seemed so artificial, non-human. He felt uneasy being alone with these two in such a confined space - suddenly her eyes hot fully open and wide and he was staring right into them - but no acknowledgement came back - it was as though there was nothing there beyond the glassy reflection.

Bang, bang, bang, bang! The whole room shuddered, and the pilot jumped with fright-

"What the fuck are you doing!" he shouted. Mandrake did not look at him, but turned to Constance instead:

"Did I startle you? I'm just trying to figure out a weak point - you carry on sleeping if you want - I'll wake you when Mother releases us-" said Mandrake, with no irony.

"It's OK - I'm awake now," answered Constance, also with no irony. The pilot felt very edgy, being trapped in this small area with these two killing machines. He never felt right around Faith Seekers - it wasn't just their ominous black armoured uniforms – or their lack of response – it was the way they were just... not human. He suddenly remembered where he had heard that name before:

"Didn't your family used to be witches?" he asked. Mandrake stopped, but did not turn and look at him or answer, but returned to his task.

"You know - pre-secular era - I heard they were witches-"

"Family?" said Mandrake, "we don't have family - you know that. We are clones. We don't have family." He realised his mistake - but at least he had elicited a response - no easy thing to start a chat with a Faith Seeker, he thought to himself, feeling a bit bolder now.

"You know what I mean - your gene pool -" he said. Mandrake turned away from the door and faced him.

"Family? Heard? Witches! You're not supposed to know anything about Faith Seekers. All areas of weakness must be eliminated - if they capture and torture you-" said Mandrake.

"I know, I know - but I won't talk," said the pilot. "If I ever get caught, I've made the decision - brain freeze pill - you never hear of a Faith Seeker being rescued from the Porcs, anyway - always crucified - always. But humans – I'm not going to be kept hostage," he said.

"If you've made your decision, stick to it - I've never seen an officer use it, but if you have no option-" Mandrake said, trailing off.

"I've seen the training viseos - plenty of people use it -

it's very quick," he said. "The tech is sound - you take a memory snap of the mind, store it, and if we are captured – we pop the pill which completely destroys all memories stored in the cerebral cortex - but all life support systems, the cerebella, the stump, all work perfectly - unaffected - like a new-born baby, innocent..." he trailed off as he realised his enthusiastic explanation was being looked at blankly by Mandrake and Constance.

"And then they put all the memories back in. Back to your old self in seconds. That's what I'm hoping for..." the pilot said, but with the enthusiasm in his voice curtailing as he felt the Faith Seekers' stare absorb it. "Well, it does work, doesn't it? I've seen the-" he was interrupted by Constance, turning ominously towards him:

"No - how could it - anyone with experience in the field could tell them that," Constance stated. Mandrake continued her explanation:

"The concept looks sound on screen - but when it's put in the real world, well, things are different there. They should have asked us," he said. "If you have to kill yourself to destroy a Porc, then that is what you should do. That pill is only designed for if you get captured and there is no possibility of escape. Last resort - if you fail!" Mandrake said the word 'fail' with contempt.

"So where does it fail? It works perfectly – the scientists have confirmed it,' said the pilot.

"Yes - but Mother is far cleverer - she understands people - she knows the flaw - the Porcs don't care that they can't get the information out - they know they can't talk - they want to torture them - they want to hurt them and crack their bones - burn their skin - tear their flesh -

whether they can feel it or not! Even a cat stops playing with a mouse once it's dead - but not the Porcs - they'll keep going long after there's no life - hanging, crucifying, displaying, warning - instilling fear into everyone - the loved ones, the innocent ones - their own children."

"And you understand that?" said the pilot.

"I understand what I need to understand. I do as Mother tells me to do."

"Yes - but you seem to understand them a bit more - it must be the witch in you." He hoped he had not annoyed him more - he just wanted to know if the rumours were true. Mandrake's reaction was not what he expected - rather than explosive, it seemed to make Mandrake contemplative. All the while, Mandrake had constantly been trying to break the seal, to find the weakness that would allow him to escape, but now he turned and gave them both his full attention.

"You and all the others have got it wrong - I'm not descended from a witch - Sunetra is," said Mandrake. He then finally sat on the relaxer and faced Constance.

"We'd just wiped out a nest of Porcs - another cellar - this country is full of them - one of these big houses in the rural zones, when I noticed the squadron leader, Sunetra, standing over one of the Porcs she had killed - well - I wondered if she had noticed anything unusual, and I went over to look. Well - Sunetra was staring at the painting on the wall. This old house - over a thousand yours old - had portraits of the owners going back all this time - and this one was the spitting image of Sunetra.

"So the woman looked like her - what's the connection?" asked Constance.

"She lifted the painting off the wall and on the back

was written the person's name - and the fact that she had been burned as a witch. That's all there is to it," said Mandrake. Constance sat still, absorbed in this description, before asking:

"And what was the name of the woman?" but was interrupted by Mandrake suddenly launching himself off the chair and kicking the seal in the door with ferocious energy: the door opened and then quickly tried to close on his foot, but was unable to - constantly sliding back and forth and bouncing back off his boot.

"I thought so - energy saving mode - it can't waste energy holding the doors tightly sealed when no one is trying to open them -so it relaxes when it thinks you have stopped trying - never let tech know what you are thinking," Mandrake said, before beckoning the pilot with his finger. The pilot got up, shocked, hesitating –

"Now hold on, this is highly irregular – I don't want any part of this-" before letting out a cry of terror as the huge black gauntleted hand of Mandrake reached out for him. Mandrake, still standing in the doorway, his foot blocking the constant attempts of the door to close, took hold of the pilot's ID badge, ripping it from his shirt. The pilot fell to the floor terrified. Constance followed Mandrake out of the door, saying:

"The pilot is correct - this is highly irregular." Mandrake made no gesture to Constance, said no word, but walked with a determined purpose out of the boarding area and towards the drone. As he walked towards it, he held up the pilot's ID badge, which was scanned, recognized and triggered the doors to open wide and lower to the floor. A warning speaker blared, and grated out the message: "Mother is aware you have left without permission. Mother has not authorised you to leave the building. You cannot board the drone!"

Mandrake boarded the drone. Watching from the holding area, Constance hesitated - she looked at the computer screen and shouted: "Inform Mother I will follow Mandrake to ensure compliance with orders," though she was unsure if she really meant that or was trying to cover herself for her actions. The computer hesitated, clearly in communication with Mother.

"You cannot board the drone yet!" it screeched harshly at them. Constance also walked straight on board. You'll never get it to fly, she thought. Mother will have disabled it already. Constance was astonished to hear the engines whine and the doors seal as Mandrake made the ship countermand all orders from Mother. Constance's helmet was suddenly filled with the sound of Mother's voice: "You are to stay with Mandrake and ensure he obeys all orders. If he deviates from his primary objective, you have full authorization to deactivate him," Mother said in her comforting voice. Constance gave confirmation:

"Of course, Mother. I will follow all instructions without hesitation," she stated quietly but firmly into the communicator. She looked over to Mandrake - despite overriding the system, and breaking through Mother's command signal, he was still struggling. The nav system was refusing to comply.

"Navigate to Faith School with recent arrivals!" ordered Mandrake.

"No recent arrivals!" stated the system flatly.

"Why don't you listen? Just wait and Mother will send you there with full authorisation," Constance asked.

"There are things I don't understand - so I want to understand them, right now," said Mandrake. He looked at the nav screen - it was blank. He had made the engines work, but without any idea of where the Faith School was located he could not possibly proceed. He wracked his brains. In the corner of his eye he could see Constance with puzzlement on her face - he tried to think through all the possibilities.

At the Mother Board, Brunthe turned to Mother with some disdain -

"Shall I order Constance to dispose of him, Mother?" He seems to have 'gone rogue' as they say. Mother chided Brunthe:

"Of course not, Brunthe - that would be an overreaction - Mandrake is a first rate FSO - he just needs controlling, as always. He needs to understand the bigger picture. He will be immovable in the drone until the correct time has arrived," said Mother.

"I'm a little concerned that he is leading others astray," stated Brunthe. Mother spoke to calm his fears:

"Constance is our watch. There is no concern," she said comfortingly. Brunthe nodded his head gently in acknowledgment and turned back to his other duties, monitoring the viseoscreen which relayed the missions across various Earth sectors.

10

Drone Override

Above the Faith School, the sister hovered and looked carefully. She knew that below them, somewhere, was Deacon. Inside the hood which billowed with the cold mountain air was darkness - only a vague shape could be seen by the glowing lights of the hover bike controls. Suddenly the shape was bathed in a red glow - the screen had lit up and flashed that Deacon had been located. The sister's hood tilted towards the empty mountainous region below - she turned and gave a signal to one of the nuns - her white gloved hand indicated that they should drop in a sweep towards the mountain. The nun looked at her, and steered the bike towards the ground - looking again for confirmation, the sister pointed her finger sharply at the ground. The nun twisted her accelerator and the bike's engine howled as it pitched at ever-increasing speed towards the ground, faster and faster until, suddenly the bike was stopped by an invisible force - slamming into nothing, yet instantly exploding, the bike bounced and burned into the air - the nun's robes flaming as she fell screaming. The sister carefully watched her burning sister's trajectory - it fell in an arc - an arc which outlined a huge semicircle of air. Carefully steering her bike, the sister hovered over the section which had been hit by the nun's bike - there was a small abrasion, a dent in thin air. She hovered closer and reached out her hand - it was like touching an invisible wall. Immediately the sister knew - this was the right place - disguised by an enormous bubble of projected camouflage - the Faith School was below - and she would make sure that they would enter it.

She gave instructions for the others to form a circle, and then, as they circled the school like vultures circle a soon dead prey, the sister gave a signal - a gesture which, with her hand spread, crossed her face. The signal and its significance was instantly known by the others, in a group, as the sisters always were in a group, they reached inside their robes and pulled out a mask. A mask which seemed the perfect latex image of a person, some male, some female but all individual. As she pulled it out could be seen on the inside of the mask not the rubber back of a synthetic mask, but the fat deposits, veins and sinews of a real face which had been torn off a living person. A strap had been attached and it was fixed over the face of the Sister. It was the face of FSO Bradbury, and was the symbol of gratified revenge; and as the screen glowed red with the indicator that Deacon had been found, the nuns glided their hover bikes out of the heavens and towards the Faith School - revenge was about to delivered.

As the twin doors to the Mother Board opened, Brunthe could tell by the fiery burnish of Mother's glow that he had been summoned as a matter of urgency.

"Brunthe - Mandrake has sabotaged the drone - it has taken off without my authorization," stated Mother.

"I will check to see how-" but he was interrupted by Mother -

"I know how - I have already reprogrammed all drones to correct this weakness" she said.

"I did suggest that perhaps Mandrake should be eliminated, Mother-" he said, before Mother cut him off again.

"I know. And I have said Constance shall be our watch-" and this time Brunthe cut off Mother-

"If he does not rid himself of her as he has with the drone pilot," he said, in a suggestive tone. Mother did not mention this in her reply:

"Mandrake has commandeered the drone, and disabled the communications unit. I am unable to monitor them," which seemed to infuse Mother's voice with irritation.

"What action would you like me to take, Mother? I could send an interceptor-" again Brunth was interrupted.

"No - no need for such drastic action. I'll send a signal to the drone - it will slow down to ensure that it does not reach the school before the Porcs - we cannot have Mandrake and Constance arriving before the Sisterhood of Tongues - sacrifices have to be made."

"Of course," said Brunthe with a sigh.

"I will, of course, turn the situation to an advantage - the drone can arrive once we successfully trace the nuns' hiding place, and then they can be heroes, arriving just in time to save the survivors."

"Very good, Mother," said Brunthe. "I'll ready a news report: 'Experienced Faith Seeker with Rookie

Rescues Children from Faith School - Many Others Lost' - shall I say how many?"

"We shall have to wait and see. We don't want to give out any inaccuracies," said Mother.

"Mother?" asked Brunthe.

"Yes?" she replied.

"Can you switch off all viseos and sayers? I don't like to see what the Porcs do to them," he said with an edge of pleading in his voice.

"Of course, Brunthe. Please understand - this is the only way - Sacrific-"

"I know," interrupted Brunthe a little too quickly - he had heard it many times before.

Jude was learning fast - in less than a day he had managed to elevate himself to the role of a 'buddy' to Josh, found himself favoured by his teacher as a caring and compassionate person, had made himself known to Deacon and had talked face to face with a Faith Seeker - even reasoning with her. Sitting atop all of this was the thing giving him the most happiness. Giving him a huge sense of confidence, vitality and purpose. Purpose in the world. He was on a journey to find his mother. Optimistic and happy, he thought that soon things were going to be alright.

"Aren't you hungry?" asked Josh; Jude had been buried so deep in his thoughts that he realised that he had not eaten any of his food. Looking down at the table he could see empty plates next to his which was full.

"Well done for eating all your food, Josh. It's important that you eat - I know how upset you are - I've been there myself, but you have to eat, to keep your strength up, to stay healthy." Josh looked at him, then looked down towards his full plate. "And I have a long journey ahead, so I have to stay strong," Jude said, partly to Josh, and partly to himself. He started to eat his food, looking at his plate, talking to himself and chatting to Josh in a breezy manner. "They do lovely food here, Josh, don't they? What do you think of this fruit? It's real - they grow it in the gardens here - part of the therapy. This is my favourite spot - couched away in the corner - I like to watch everyone, see what's going on - everyone dashing about - and I'm watching them all - and they can't see me! We're in our secret den here, Josh!" He suddenly realised he had talked a lot and was getting no response - "Josh?" He turned towards him, and saw that look of terror again. Josh was frozen again, save for the flaring nostrils as once again he was struggling to breath. "What is it? What's the matter?" He followed Josh's eyes across the breakfast hall - people moving, trolleys rolling, laughing, shouting - what was it, he thought? And then his darting eyes registered a dark shadow: unseen, shaded in a dark recess at the back. Until you kept your eyes still and stared, and allowed them to turn the brightness down, you would never have seen it. Sitting there, upright, dark - almost invisible - was the brooding figure of the Faith Seeker.

"It's alright. I don't think she's going to hurt us," said Jude. He put a reassuring arm around Josh, patting him and showing him how to control his breathing - "Nice and slow, through the nose," said Jude, never taking his eyes of the Faith Seeker watching them. As the figure rose, Jude wondered whether he should call for help, but the figure seemed to read his mind, and raised a hand with a finger pointing in a way which seemed to mean 'no - don't do it'. It was then that Jude knew it was the same Faith Seeker who had been in the bedroom the previous night. Coming into the light, he could see it was Sunetra. She walked purposefully across the canteen and then loomed over them, her shadow upon their faces, until Jude said-

"Are you going to sit with us?" Sunetra moved into the corner, positioning herself so that she was in the darkness, with her back against the wall and her eyes scanning all around. For a minute, nothing was said; nothing happened, nothing was done.

"Do you like sitting in the corner, too? Hidden away? So that you can see everyone but they can't see you?" asked Jude.

"Yes," she answered. With no more of a reply than that, Jude said:

"Then we have something in common. I like to see the people, but I like to keep myself to myself." Jude said.

"You have to be careful," answered Sunetra tentatively.

"What do you want?" asked Jude after some time. Sunetra felt awkward, disoriented. It was not a feeling she was used to. She had placed herself in a position which was alien to her. Her FSO uniform was decommissioned, she had no weapons, no protective clothes and she was sitting having breakfast with Porc children.

"I said, what do you want?" Jude repeated.

"Fruit, fresh and dried. Cereal, mixed grains. Protein compound, milk, toast," she answered.

11

Confession

Sunetra stayed in the shadows, and Jude brought the food she asked for. He put it down in front of her, and then sat next to Josh again, moving away his uneaten food. The breakfast area was emptying fast now as people moved towards the learning zones. They were left alone. Alone, perhaps, but above, in the shadows, hovered a micro drone, zooming in, adjusting position, capturing all the fine nuances of the relationship which was forming at the table; and all being fed back to the Mother Board. All being monitored by Brunthe, whose eyes darted back and forth between Deacon at his prayers and the scene unfolding between Sunetra and the two children. He asked for sound on this scene.

"When I lived at home, before…" Jude broke off, not wanting to utter the words about the terrible experience of losing his mother.

"I know, before you lost your mother…" said Sunetra - she noticed Jude's eyes flash a little darkly - she was trained to pick up on hostile body language to anticipate flash points, and had to remind herself not to respond with a pre-emptive strike.

The viseodrone zoomed in close and far away Brunthe saw the flash of darkness in Jude's eyes - he let out a little sigh of concern to himself. 'Be careful, Sunetra, this is an area of which you know little. You have never been trained for this - relationships are alien to you - you have never had them, and you were not made for them. Be careful', thought Brunthe to himself.

"My friend told me that Faith Seekers were not human, that they were robots made by Mother. Is that true? Are you a robot?" asked Jude. It was Sunetra's turn for her eyes to flash a little darkly, before sidling up closer to him, and putting her arm out towards him - both Jude and Josh pulled back in fear - but, putting one arm around Josh to comfort him, he reached out and touched Sunetra's hand.

"Do I feel like a robot?" she whispered. There was an undertone of hope in her tone. The tension was palpable, but receded when Jude said, after some thought:

"No. I think you are a person. Just like me."

Watching on the viseo screen, Brunthe sighed and tutted, "Dearie me. Oh, Dearie me," he said to himself, "Of course you are a robot, Sunetra."

Jude reached into his pocket and brought out his memory card. Sunetra noticed that the area marked 'Family' had been iris-locked - Jude stared into it to unlock the section. He flicked through various photos and found a picture of himself with his mother, father, himself and a large white dog.

"That's her," he said. "That's my mother." Sunetra

thought carefully, and did not utter a response other than to say-

"Who's he?" pointing her finger at the dog.

"She. She's a girl. Her name was Stella. She was my friend," said Jude as he looked deep into the picture.

"She is beautiful," said Sunetra simply. By now, even Josh was relaxing, and joined in with:

"She is beautiful - I would love a dog like that! Where is she now? Is she at home? Can we go and see her?" he asked. A deep sigh signalled the words to follow.

"She's dead. They killed her," said Jude. Sunetra knew straight away who 'they' were - she had done it herself many times.

"Oh, did she try to protect you?" she asked.

"Yes - I miss her. Dad said, one day, when this is all over, we'll have a new one. But I'm not sure," said Jude with doubt in his voice.

"Can't you get any more like her?" asked Josh.

"Yes, but she, you know, she won't be Stella. You can't just replace her. If someone is gone, you can't just put another one there and it's the same - like they *are* the same. Can you?" asked Jude, who noticed that Sunetra had been nodding her head in agreement with the sentiment. It was quiet for a few moments, a contemplative silence, when Sunetra said:

"Well... let me tell you a secret..." Jude looked up and put his ear closer to her lips to hear Sunetra's whispered confession. He never dreamed he would be so near to a Faith Seeker and live.

Above, the quiet whirr of electric motors could be heard as the viseo drone jostled for a clearer view of her lips, and extended its gain settings on the microphone to maximum.

"When I was a child, my mother bought me a puppy -
I used to tease him with my teddy bear-" started
Sunetra. Far away in the mother board, Brunthe angled
his head to hear clearly above the noise of interference
and then raised an eyebrow at the mention of Sunetra
being a child: 'Oh, Dearie me - what an imagination you
have, Sunetra. 'When you were a child,' indeed." He
pulled out an oblong object made of paper - a notebook.
It was the only way in this day and age to ensure
secrecy. To ensure that nothing could be intercepted -
there was only one copy, only one report, only one
person who had written it. He wrote the words, in
pencil, 'Report on Sunetra for Mother,' and underneath
he made a list: 'fantasising; positive affection;
imagination; caring; empathy'.

Jude laughed at the tale Sunetra had just told him -
"Did he really?" he asked.

"Yes - even though, years later, when he had grown
from a pup, and he clearly knew that Ted Bear was -
that's his toy bear's name-" Sunetra explained.

"I guessed that!" Jude said.

"You did? Of course. Even though he knew he was
not real - he would still guard over his food, react out of
jealousy and, boy - if you go to give him a treat and Ted
is near-" said Sunetra before having her sentence
finished:

"He'd get you!" laughed Jude. On the viseoscreen, the
sight looked strange - a Faith Seeker with two Porc
children engaged in playful talk.

"I've often thought it's a bit like religion," Sunetra
said.

"What do you mean?" replied Jude, suddenly a little

tense.

"Well - he's not stupid - my dog-"

"The dog you had when you were a child?" prompted Jude.

"Yes - well, he knows if something is real, if it's alive - and yet, because I've constantly acted as if Ted is real, a real living thing which would steal his treats and toys, he - well, he just seems to believe it. My acting as if Ted is real makes him believe that he is..." Sunetra was instantly aware of the hostile sensations again: "Are you OK, Jude?" she asked, noticing that Jude seemed to be withdrawing from her. He had put his head down slightly and continued to talk without looking at her.

"I thought you were my friend," he said. Sunetra went to go near him but he flinched from her.

"I am your friend - what have I done?" she asked in genuine puzzlement.

"You're teaching me," he said contemptuously. "Instead of being my friend, you're teaching me. You're tricking religion into everything - it's getting in the way of our friendship. I don't like being tricked." Sunetra thought carefully again.

"I'm sorry, Jude. I wasn't doing that on purpose. I promise you. I was just telling you something I think," she said with urgency in her voice. "It's just, well, you sound like the teachers here. They make friends and then do fun things with you - and then they turn it in to religion - it's always religion!" He said with contempt in his voice.

"I see. But that's their job - that's why they are here-" but she was cut off-

"You sound like them! You are just the same as them!" he shouted at her.

"Them?" asked Sunetra.

"Yes - the Deacon and the Fathers and all the others in Holy Place - where I used to go with my...my m..." he stumbled. Sunetra tried to judge the situation, but she felt that this was beyond her capabilities.

"I understand. You've been through it all your life - and now you're having to go through it all again - but learning the opposite - un-learning-" she urged.

"It's called 'Demystifying', they say. Getting rid of all the lies. Wiping out the fantasy and replacing it with the truth, that's what they say," he said with anger and confusion in his voice.

"I know. I'm not doing that - I'm just chatting as a friend. I promise. I want you to trust me. That's why I'm telling you about my dog. I'm sorry about your suffering. If your mother hadn't taken you to those churches you would never have had to go through this-" Sunetra immediately realised she had touched a raw nerve. The mention of the signifier, Jude's mother, caused him to flinch, and something welled up, forcing his body to rise from the chair and confront her. He looked at her with fury.

"It's not her fault! Stop blaming everything on her!" he stated firmly. Before Sunetra could respond, Jude had taken Josh's hand, and they turned and were running away from her - running to the door.

"Jude!" Sunetra called out pleadingly. He stopped, turned around and said:

"And I didn't lose my mother - she didn't leave me - she was taken from me," said Jude, with a fixed stare of determination at Sunetra, "Taken away by people like you!" He ran, and would not stop.

"Mother?" Brunthe stood in the amphitheatre of the Mother Board - all was dark. The dais started to emit a glowing light which grew until Mother became corporeal, bathing the whole room in warm light.

"Yes, Brunthe?" she asked, her voice comforting.

"I am concerned that protocols have been broken," he said simply.

"Oh, dear - that is very worrying. What has happened?" she asked in her usual, comforting, but concerned voice.

"It's Sunetra. She has delayed coming back on duty and has befriended two young Porcs at the Faith School." In his hand, the little paper notebook was pressed tightly closed between his fingers, which gripped and re-gripped the covers, as if unable to find a comfortable hold.

"I see. Order her to report back on duty immediately. She is not to form friendships. She is not a teacher - she is a Faith Seeker. She is to leave immediately. Tell her. I do not want her there when the school is breached - it is important that we let them win a battle, Brunthe. We need to trace them to their nest," Mother said with some determination. Brunthe nodded, and put the paper notebook back into his pocket.

"Is there anything else on your mind, Brunthe?" asked Mother with some concern.

"She - I mean Sunetra made some, some perceptive remarks about cognitive and psychological tendencies in children," he said with some hesitation. His hand patted the outside of his jacket pocket, just to check that the pocket book was still there.

"Yes. Sunetra is a very perceptive and intelligent woman - a most exemplary and brave officer, sacrificing much in the servi-"

"She has, indeed. She has sacrificed much, Mother-" interrupted Brunthe.

"Yes - but remember, Brunthe - do not become attached to her - she was born to make sacrifices. You know that," said Mother with emphasis on the word 'you' to ensure he understood his complicity.

"Oh, yes - of course, Mother. I am fully aware that she, as are all the clones, born to follow this path. It's just that it is touching to see them reaching out like that," he said.

"It is indeed, Brunthe - I understand fully - no matter how carefully their genes are constructed and their conditioning implanted, they are, after all, made from the same material as humans. And they naturally tend towards human needs. But quickly, Brunthe - ensure she is not at the Faith School - she will have to sacrifice again, of course, but not this time," said Mother.

12

The Faith School Attacked

The teachers were wrong. The children who played in the grounds and parks of the Faith School with such exuberance and spirit were suddenly muted into a sombre silence. After all they had been brought up to believe, and were now in the process of unbelieving, the children could only think that the teachers were wrong. That there really was a god after all - for a mighty clap of thunder shook the Earth and the sun went dim. Like a full eclipse of the moon, the insects, the birds, the animals, and the people knew that something was not right with the world; the eeriness and stillness of the air compelled them to look upwards in a reverential silence, bearing witness as the azure sky darkened and cracked.

Sunetra's training channelled her instincts - the deep, rumbling thunder, so deep it felt as though the Earth itself were shaking, rose up through her body, transforming her back into the fighting machine for which she was created. She fell to the floor and, hidden amongst the plants, she surveyed and gathered information - it was clearly the sky which was the source of the thunderous noise. She snaked into a clearing amongst the trees to get a better view. She felt naked and vulnerable without her uniform - she had no tech, no comms, no weapons - she felt alone and cornered. Around her the silencing of voices became palpable.

Jude was silent, too. Only a short distance from Sunetra, Jude had run into the gardens, taking his anger out by climbing the highest tree he could find, and, losing himself in the dense foliage he hid, and watched. He watched Sunetra looking for him and thought that perhaps, if he climbed high enough, he would be safe, hidden from her. He climbed - higher and higher, for safety, looking down on the danger below. However, his natural instincts did not serve him well this time. No - the danger this time was from high above. Feeling the thunder, seeing the sky dim and even the Faith Seeker woman fall and hide below him, he clung to the tree in terror.

Sunetra sprang and pounced through the shrubs and plants, and as she reached the end of the gardens, with the buildings in sight, she stopped, flipping herself over to look at the sky and take stock. The thunderous sounds she now identified - explosives, bombs of some type - possibly Cavern Crackers - used to penetrate the deeps caves Porcs often hide themselves in. She could tell it would only be a matter of time before they penetrated. She ran to the building, sprinting and dodging through the panic-stricken and terrified crowds which now blocked her way; Sunetra tried shouting 'Faith Seeker - everyone move' but people were more frightened of the world above.

All were held still by the fascination of what was

happening - as if they had all been caught in the gaze of Medusa herself, and turned to stone. It was a scene of terror - unable to run, teachers and mothers and fathers held on to the hands of children in their care, awestruck by the unknown horrors about to be unleashed.

Suddenly, in what seemed like a thunderbolt from the gods, the sky cracked, the clouds darkened and the sun dimmed lower. Then, the crack became jagged like an eggshell cracking, with angular sections falling and hitting the floor and trees like crumbling plaster from a cathedral in an earthquake - after all, the beautiful creation of the sky in the faith school was just as much a work of art as the creation of the heavenly skies in the cathedrals of old, except this, of course, was done with much more verisimilitude. Fascination and surprise made them look upwards. This school, this environment, this world - created with such care and attention to provide those in it with a feeling of serenity, of safety, of comfort and inner calmness was being ripped apart. And like a giant skull viciously cracked open, the precious ethereality of consciousness would be sucked out and replaced with a virulent and visceral creed.

Sunetra now weaved her way through the crowds and finally entered the rest room - there she frantically pulled on her uniform, frustrated that it would not restart until she closed the hinges, scanned her retinas - and all the time hitting start, start, start! Finally, her uniform gave the high-pitched whirring, comms packs went online and, most importantly, her weapons reacted to her touch. Her gun gave its reassuring whine as it charged to full capacity. She made her way back to the playgrounds, now fully armoured.

Suddenly the whole sky gave up its pretence and revealed itself for what it was - the giant viseoscreen which arched over this fabricated land froze in a still frame. The clouds stopped moving, the sun stopped shining. There was an enormous boom as the crack was widened by an explosion- and through the crack was darkness. Blackness. The blackness of the night sky outside, starless and deep.

Through the crack came the very creature which had turned everyone to stone - with her green-hued skin and empty-eyed sockets came Medusa with her Gorgon sisters, followed by streams of followers, flying through the crack into the capacious vault. The Faith School had been breached and the sisters had entered.

Alarms pierced the still air, red lights flashed across the faces of the terrified and confused. Warnings were blared out:

"Emergency! Emergency! We have been breached - Call Mother, call Mother. Emergency! Emergency!" Small drones transmitting Mother's voice came through the erratically bobbing sayers:

"I have heard you - help is on its way - I have dispatched drones - they will be with you in minutes. People of Religious Conviction - I address you - please do not hurt us - we have extended mercy and only eliminated those who continue to dissent."

Sunetra, hearing Mother's recorded voice over the speakers repeatedly tried to get her comms to work - but no response came but static. She watched and assessed for a moment before her ears pricked to a different sound. No matter how many times she heard them, it still sent a wrenching feeling through her stomach - she felt that familiar and sudden jump of her heart, followed by the rise in breathing rate and tingling all over her body - she felt a sudden gasp in her mouth, a choking sensation, the start of a cry, with water filling her eyes just enough to start tipping over into tears - 'adrenaline response' she thought - all correct; the sounds came again - unearthly screams, pitched female, yet unhuman. The sky darkened as the crack splintered further under the force of blows hitting the sky.

Jude heard the screams around him, saw the world starting to change, the sun growing dim, the things falling from the sky. He felt unreal, like it was happening to someone else - that he was watching a viseofilm. All around him the screams of terror, the wailing. Little robots whizzed through the sky, shouting and giving directions. He arched his head to try and see what was happening through the foliage, but it was difficult to clearly understand the nature of the event. He clung to the branches of the tree, sitting firmly. The tree he was in had been perfect for climbing. It was twisted and gnarled, the branches multitudinous and criss-crossing. It was heavy with fruit, the red orbs glowing in batches around him. A drone suddenly whizzed by, stopped and looked into the tree, seeming to bob and peer through the branches. It was scanning - it knew there was someone there. It floated slowly through the branches, and stopped. Jude kept as still as death, his heart beating fast, but trying to breathe only through his nose, not to make much noise. Jude wondered what it was going to do to him. It's little iris suddenly opened wide as if in alarm. Jude heard the crackle of electricity as a bolt hit it and it exploded in a ball of flames. He closed his eyes to shield them from the flash, turning his head to see a black and white figure approaching the tree at great speed. The next moment he was falling through the branches, landing at the base of the tree with a thump. Branches, leaves and fruit fell around and on him. The black and white figure floated down to him, and through the haze of a bumped head, he could see the cowled face bending down to look at him, before a hand started to reach out.

"Leave him! He is mine!" a voice said. A voice which he felt he knew. A figure in orange walked towards him: "It's alright, Jude. Remember me?" The figure of Deacon towered above him. He reached into the tree and pulled down one of the lower branches, plucking one of the bright red orbs of fruit. He rubbed it clean on his overalls, before taking a large, crunching bite of the apple. He chewed for a moment, before looking down at Jude, smiled and said, "Mmmm… delicious."

Jude picked himself up and ran, ran as fast as he could. Even through the discordance in the air, Jude could hear Deacon's voice in mockery of the recorded pleas from Mother: "Please don't hurt us, please don't hurt us," intoned whiningly.

The alarms which were sounding through the sayers were suddenly silenced. All the sayers, viseobots, and guides which were blaring instructions for the children and people to find safety, what to do to protect themselves, lighting up to show the way to escape, were suddenly silent, and then fell to the floor as if their invisible strings had been cut. An eerie silence bode all to stay still and their skin began to pimple as the warmth of the created summer's day was sucked out through the crack in the sky. The sun went out. It flickered back on for a moment as the emergency circuits tried in vain to relight it, but then nothing. All cowered and looked up towards the open dome with its ever-widening crack leaving in a cold winter's light.

Suddenly startled by the sound of demonic horns, the pupils were suddenly aware of black figures flying though the sky, their hooded cloaks flowing behind them. People were horror struck, and could only watch as hundreds of these figures flew around the ruptured sky like some macabre vision of an ancient hollowed night. As the figures moved closer and closer to the ground, their faces became discernible. Josh cowered in terror, huddled with his friends, sinking themselves into play pits, the sand, anywhere where they could find a way to try and get away from the sight unfolding before them. Josh saw one of the black hooded figures spiral down near enough for him to see - and he was horrified that the face, though distorted and flapping, was the face of someone he recognised. A Faith Seeker who had brought him here previously. It swooped down ever closer, until it swooshed above him, the flapping flanges of skin loosely causing the face to billow in the wind. Horrified, Josh found he could not breath, and felt himself helplessly pass out as he was lifted into the air.

Sunetra was shocked to find all tech immobilised; had seen her gun power down, and fail to respond. She had never experienced this infiltration of their technology before. She had run to Jude's room, though unsure why - and looked in to the darkness but could see nothing for a moment - then she thought she could see a shape under the bed - entering the room a familiar voice came from behind her.

"Surprise!" said Deacon, as he slashed at her with a knife. It sparked off her uniform, and Sunetra instantly twisted, knocked and punched forward. Two nuns came out of the darkness and grabbed her arms - easily strong enough to overpower them, Sunetra used their strength to launch both feet into the air in a flying kick at Deacon, all four bodies hitting the floor. Out of the nuns' grip she flew towards Deacon, who lifted up her gun and pointed it directly at her. To her astonishment it lit up with power. Deacon smiled and, as she was desperately trying to find ways of assessing the situation without her tech, she was momentarily distracted by the screams of terror from outside the room. She suddenly felt her hair being yanked and her head and neck pulled backwards. She could see out of the corner of her eye that as soon as Deacon held the gun, the light had come back on - it had re-armed at his touch - she thought to allow him to think he was in a position of power and then wait for her moment to take him down. Now was her chance. As her head was pulled back towards him she escalated the velocity beyond what he would expect, and head butted him full in the face - he jerked his hand involuntarily and the gun fired into the ceiling several times. She flipped around and grabbed her gun while ensuring that his hand was holding it to keep it activated. She was stronger than him, and twisted his wrist around, bending his arm back till the gun was only inches from his face. She squeezed his finger on the trigger, but could not get her finger at the right angle, blocked by the trigger guard. Deacon fought back with the ferocity which comes from knowing your opponent's only aim is to blow your brains out there and then.

They rolled on the floor, her head was still woozy from the head-butt, and as they locked in a battle of strength, Deacon realised his best hope of survival was to throw away Sunetra's gun. He threw it and then threw himself fully on top of Sunetra - rolling over until he was almost gaining the upper hand. Sunetra felt his weight across her, but could feel that his arms were shaking, his muscles would not last much longer - she took in a deep breath, ready to knock him from her, when she saw the door open and an FSO walk in. With relief, she eased her grip - and looked up to see that it was Bradbury - an officer she had known for many years. Sunetra's eyes then widened as she realised that this Bradbury was heavily wounded - she tried to see what was wrong - Bradbury was pale, and the skin looked bloodless - as the face peered down on her, the flanges of skin flapped and flopped, and blood dripped from his face on to hers. Sunetra stared with disconcertion - it was a dead face, but the eyes were alive - the eyes were intently staring at her with hatred - but they were not the eyes of Bradbury. The face had been torn off and was being used as a mask - a mask to confuse, horrify and terrorise all who saw it. The person wearing Bradbury's face raised its cloaked arm and hit her unconscious.

13

Sacrifices Have to be Made

Chaos reigned in The Faith School - children ran in horror and confusion as the Sisters wearing the faces of the dead Faith Seekers they had slaughtered set about the destruction of the school with a fervency born out of pure hatred. With no one able to offer resistance the black and white nuns, resembling medieval woodcuts in their bloodless appearance, went about with little resistance, destroying all before them, setting alight all that would burn, smashing all that would break, and killing all who would could not escape. In the end, a chosen band of people were caged and held ready, wishing they had died a quick death and not fought for survival.

Sunetra's mind slowly floated through the clouds of consciousness. The darkness lifted, and her mind floated faster, until she opened her eyes and light pierced into her skull with a searing intensity. She blinked rapidly, her training coming to the fore as her consciousness returned. Immediately, she surveyed her condition and then the immediate area. She was feeding the information into her comms pack - "Regained perceptions. Immobilised. Head wound. All electronics immobilized..." with that, she shook her head and realized that she was talking to herself. She was not wearing her uniform, she had no comms pack to talk into. She was stripped to her underwear and was tied and trussed like an animal on a stick. With her realization came the emotions - old emotions. Memories of things past, portends of things to come. She started to breathe heavily through her nose, and felt herself feeling sick with adrenalin. Thoughts of past hurt came into her mind and she heard herself say: "Please, no, please don't" even though she had never said those things: she was a Faith Seeker - she would never say those things; so why did she think she had, she wondered? What made her despair with these memories, though, was not that she could not bear the pain, but that she would not talk. She would never betray Mother. And that meant she had to endure the pain which was to come.

She wondered if she would survive this one. She always wondered that. And then, as the beating, and cutting, and burning started, something swelled, from so deep inside her it was like she was connecting with the soul of the earth, and drawing deeply, as from a well, the strength rising up inside and filling her. But she now felt that this inner strength was not fathomless, as she had always felt it to be, but that there was a limit - whether the limit was because of her slowly failing body, she did not know - perhaps there was a limit, a limit placed by the earth, or by some unknown process. But she knew the limit would, at some point, be reached. And then she would have done her duty for the last time.

Sunetra was brought back to the present moment by the screams around her. Deacon was with the Sister who had rescued him. Between them they were commanding a rapid and precise ordering of the chaos which had been brought down upon the school. The nuns were clearing the area of any evidence of their violence. They then started attaching viseocams to themselves. A tableau was created. Wooden crosses were erected. He could see a child of about eight cowering behind the swings in the playground - he walked over and held out his hand. The boy was, of course, still too terrified to come out while the Ghost Faith Seeker was there. The child came forward, "Ah, Josh! I see you are safe! That's excellent! Come with me," said Deacon. Even though he was gripped with terror, there was something in the way Deacon held out his hand and smiled that caused him to obey.

"Good. Now - I think it's time for you to be reunited. With your brother, your mother and your father - all together again in the arms of our Lord. Come with me!" Deacon whispered conspiratorially in his ear as he took hold of the confused and hyperventilating Josh, marching him towards the construction of wooden pillars.

All the children were rounded up and taken away by the nuns - Deacon shouted across to adults, the parents, the teachers, so that the children could hear too - the nuns ran, holding the children's hands, to safety. He handed over Josh to the nuns, ensuring his hands was gripped firm by the grasping hands of the nuns.

"To safety - lead all the little ones to safety!" he shouted. As soon as they had left Deacon set about organising events with practised efficiency. His voice now changed, his contorted demeanour and became that of a zealot, an intense and evil well of hatred.

"Martyr them!" he ordered, pointing to the parents, teachers and carers who had just been taken away. Deacon climbed aboard the back of a hover bike, orchestrating the nuns and the whole scene like a film director flying above the action below. Within minutes, the large wooden crosses which had been erected trembled with the blows of hammers as people were nailed to them. Petrol was thrown over the crosses. Deacon said to the Sister:

"I know we do not have much time - I know they are on their way - this has to be done quickly!" They then went about positioning and setting up their camera shots, strategically placing a dead child here, a mutilated one, decorating the set as would a butcher with their shop window display the carefully cleaved meat to its best advantage - the full scope of the Faith School massacre could be seen.

"A single drone is on its way - an unauthorised one - rescue party is not due to arrive for another 30 minutes," informed the sister to Deacon.

"Quick, hurry!" he replied, "just finish the video - leave them, everybody go…" The nuns and Deacon took up their positions. Deacon looked across at Sunetra and smiled. He walked over to her, pulling out a knife from his boot. She flinched. She did not think it would start now. Surly he was not going to just kill her here, like this? She was too valuable. He started to cut at his clothes, and then to tear them, ripping with his hands. He fell to his knees, then the floor, rolling in the earth beside her, convulsing and throwing himself into the ground. When his appearance was that of someone who had been to hell and back, he strode over to the crosses, reached up to one woman who was begging for mercy, and said to her: "It will come, my child. I will give you mercy very soon." She cried, saying,

"But I am one of you - you know me - we prayed together - I risked everything," she sobbed.

"I know, my child. I know," he said gently. Deacon remembered the words of the priest again "Befriend and betray!" Deacon remembered those words from all those years ago - and he was grateful, for they had turned out to be wise words indeed. What a wise old man he had been. He suddenly cried out: "I am directed by God!" And with that, he twisted her foot around the nail, so that the blood oozed and ran down his arm. As she screamed, so did he scream - in some sort of macabre companionship - and smeared the blood over his clothes and body.

He looked up to the sisters - and gave the signal. They switched on their viseocams. Deacon pulled out a lighter from his pocket and held up the naked flame - he saw the terror in the eyes of the crucified. Retreating to a safe distance, he threw the flame, which ignited and billowed up around the crucified figures in orange fireball, before crackling, spitting and lapping around the still-screaming bodies, the wooden crosses blackening as the bodies melted into them.

The sisters flew down, to film the sobbing Deacon acting out scenes of despair - trying to save the people from their horrific torture. He cried and screamed: "Please help them -please! The Faith Seekers - they did this to us - I managed to run away, but my brothers and sisters! Oh, my Lord God − not the children!" The footage was captured and Deacon ordered everyone to leave. Their work had been done. He pointed to Sunetra, ordering that she be brought, before they left in a swarm, rising above the scenes of devastation below, the black smoke billowing in circles as the hover bikes rushed upwards. The verisimilitude to a film set was uncanny - only there were no actors and pyrotechnics - all was real, the sets, the props and the people; yet the tale which would be told from it would be an intricately carved conceit of propaganda.

Mandrake pushed the engines as hard as they would go - he then smashed the safety computer to override it and push the engines even further. The whining and pitch screamed even through the hull of the drone, which now reverberated with the increasingly unstable engines. Locked in concentration, Mandrake suddenly realised that the voice calling his name over and over through noise of the screaming engines was real - Constance was pointing her hand at the viseoscreen. Looking across, Mandrake could see a renegade signal breaking though the official broadcasting channel.

"It's the Faith School!" said Constance. A face, clad in religious garments, kindly, old and with a profoundly sad expression, addressed the camera directly.

"People of the world - today, we attempted to rescue our beloved families from one of your official torture camps you call 'Faith Schools'. We managed to gain access when all Faith Seekers and staff fled after setting the school ablaze. We tried to save the innocent children and people there, but it was too late for most. The scenes of horror we found there were unbearable! We show you the viseo capture from their own security cameras." The screen now showed what looked like security camera footage - it showed the sisters and nuns running into the school, horrified at the sight of the burning bodies on the crosses. Two nuns could be seen helping a heavily bleeding Deacon to walk from his cell - at the sight of the screaming people on the cross, he ran over, desperately trying to put out the flames and rescue them. He was pulled back by the nuns for his own safety. It was clear that the flames had taken the lives of all there. Scattered around were the bodies of children, mothers trying to protect them. The screen showed him go up to one of the burned crucifixes and tenderly take down the limp body of a small child of about 8 years and weep. He carried the body with tenderness and respect, as might a father with a lost child, before raging at the viseocam:

"Look what they have done to our people - tortured, humiliated and killed us in the most awful mockery of our Lord the Saviour - our own brothers and sisters - how could a civilised society do this to innocent people? Look at yourselves! question what your leaders are doing - is this what you want? Is this what you want done in your name?" He fell to the floor and wept, holding the burned and mutilated body of the child in his arms, while the flames rose around him. Cutting back to the kindly old priest, in the background could be seen Deacon weeping, being helped to walk by the two sisters. "Why? Why?" he asked, shaking his head back and forth. Mandrake flicked the viseoscreen off.

"Mother's taking her time terminating the transmission," said Constance. Mandrake did not comment, but continued to wrestle with the controls of the increasingly unpredictable drone.

"We're here - get ready for landing - full assault

mode-" but his list of prep checks was interrupted by Constance-

"I know what to do, Mandrake! Equipment ready. Weapons armed-" but Mandrake interrupted her -

"Good idea to use caution - but they're long gone. Just look out for booby traps," he said.

The drone passed through the smoke trails, descending and landing clumsily − over-fast and unsteady, it hit the ground with a crunch, lifted and dented by large rocks it gave a curiously unsteady wobble. Still in motion, the ramp descended, not quite reaching the ground. Inside, Constance was readying herself to drop down the landing ramp when Mandrake stopped her. He indicated upwards, and they both climbed the ladder to the escape hatch on the roof, sliding down the back of the drone and dropping to the floor behind.

There was no need for any of the precautions; at the entrance to the Faith School, Mandrake and Constance carefully stayed in formation, covering each other, checking for any possible danger - booby-traps, snipers - there were none. Deacon and the sisters had left exactly what they wanted - a scene of horror, torture and terror to forever show as evidence of the evil of Mother and the people who act on her behalf.

"Do you think the people will believe them?" asked Constance, looking at the battered and bloody bodies of the teachers lying on the singed grass.

"I don't know - we need to concentrate on our job. All that stuff is the Mother Board's job." Mandrake frantically looked through the piles of dead and burning bodies, checking for signs of something - something he was looking for.

"I think you are right - I don't think there is anyone left alive - perhaps we should-" started Constance, before Mandrake turned and snarled angrily at her:

"We do what we have to do - look for Sunetra - we have a duty to always look after our fellow officers!" Mandrake marched off, not waiting for Constance and she stood looking after him, thinking that his desire so save Sunetra was far beyond what would normally be acceptable.

Picking through the dead bodies, waiting for their comms packs to go back online, they were startled by the sudden burst of static from the speakers. All tech was now restarting in their uniforms, and Mandrake, after anxiously waiting for precious seconds for the system to be usable, immediately scanned the area - it bleeped steadily, showing no sign of Sunetra. Standing amongst the smoking bodies and congealing blood, both Faith Seekers looked up as the speakers jumped back to life, broadcasting a loop of Deacon's mocking, whiny imitation of Mother's plea:

"Please don't hurt us, please don't hurt us!"

14

The Thing Inside

They say that Faith Seekers don't have souls - that they are genetically engineered not to have one. Faith Seekers are tanks: they are incredibly strong, and powerful and fierce; they are relentless and will never stop until they have destroyed all those who believe in a god. But inside, they are empty. Hollow - as they should be; that is how they were designed – hollowed out - the emptiness inside them is the room for the controller: and the controller is Mother.

But Sunetra had developed a fault and was malfunctioning. For some time now, she had felt something growing. Deep inside her, it was growing. She did not know how it had got there; but it was growing larger all the time, expanding and filling up the emptiness inside her. And then it started throbbing, rhythmically, deep inside her; she was becoming aware of new feelings – worry - she was becoming more and more worried: worried that it would show; worried that the swelling inside her could not be contained.

Inside the darkness of the body-bag, as she was dragged by her captors deep into the unknown, Sunetra thought about this. She thought about her secret, and about how she longed to see the one who she first shared this with. He was hidden; he was safe; a friend looked after him for her. When she had rest and recuperation period, she would slip away to this secret place unnoticed. And she would see him. And the *way* he looked at her. It was so overwhelming; and she knew that these feelings were never meant for her – were never meant for any Faith Seeker - *they* were there to serve Mother, and inside was nothing but emptiness. A tank framed from bone and powered by blocks of muscle, driven in single-purpose pursuit – indomitable. But inside she had always been hollow. She knew that. They had always been told that. But the thing growing inside her would not stop, and grew and grew until it had grown so large that it could not be contained in her body. It had to come out. And it did. She didn't know how this could be. There was no explanation that she knew for this. It just was.

The thing inside her grown and throbbed and grown. It had become so large that she felt it could not be contained - she was worried that it would expand and blow outside of her body, showering everyone with its force. And she knew that, although this would not be a *bad* thing, not really, but that it would be a *wrong* thing. Wrong because of who she was and where she was. But not wrong really. But Sunetra had felt the thing growing inside her till she was worried there would be no room for Mother inside. And that was when, even though she was so strong and fierce and clever, and unafraid, that was when she cried. There was nowhere to hide. Her helmet was off. She was in a room with another FSO and she could not control herself or run away. Water ran from her eyes and her nose and her mouth and her lips quivered and her legs began to buckle. Her breathing became a deep gulping. The other Faith Seeker was not at all alarmed. He immediately took control of the situation. He started first-med - recovery, scan, he gave her the words you must do in first med to ensure the patient remains calm. "Irregular heartbeat - breathing response, analysing adrenalin and pain sectors" and all those other measurements designed to let the patient know that they were being properly medicined. But that was when he became hesitant, confused, he clearly did not know what these symptoms were - he was about to reach for his helmet to call for med-aid when he looked, accidentally, into her eyes. He recognized all the symptoms - dilated pupils, running tears, redness - they all indicated possible poison, or physiological responses to trauma, but this was nothing that he had ever seen in a Faith Seeker before. But he had seen it, sometimes, in the faces of those he had killed. That was when they both realised that something was happening and that it must be kept secret. Secret from every other FSO, from all superiors - even from Mother herself.

15

Mother of Mercy

Cowering under his bed, in the darkness, the hammering of Jude's heart drummed his ears - and the more he tried to still it, the more his breathing became louder, faster, till the sheets hanging over the edge of the bed were suddenly torn away: even though just cotton sheets, they seemed to him a shield, to offer some protection, but now, under the bed, the open oblong frame became the entrance for a nightmare; and slowly, slowly, a black and white hood filled the frame. Two skeletal hands lifted the hood, and the cowl was dropped to reveal the wizened, bloodless mask of a face - a real face, ripped off someone's skull, and now attached to this creature, whose own eyes peeped through the hollow sockets with a zealot intensity which was almost glutinous - the hands reached under the bed and all went black.

"There!" said Mother - "You see the face on this nun, Brunthe? I think I have found a connection with this sister who is taking that boy." Back at the Mother Board, Brunthe and Mother were analysing the security tapes from the attack at the Faith School, running through the security viseo at great speed, she then slowed it down and played relevant sections on the viseocreen; Brunthe looked carefully, and slightly tilted his head in concentration - a young boy of about 12 is cowering terrified, and passes out as of one of the attacking sisters pulls back her hood to reveal the dead face attached to it.

"Yes - one of our FSOs, of course. I'm not sure which one…" said Brunthe. Mother's hologram looked concentrated, before she said:

"It is…" she paused for a moment, her image portraying the impression of trying to remember, while she ran facial recognition software over all the many thousands of Faith Seeker Officers who have been killed over the years. "Ah, yes - Bradbury. FSO Bradbury," she said with a tone of satisfaction - though this soon died away in an abrupt cadence, however, as Mother realised she could get no significance from this knowledge. There was a pause, a lull. Mother dimmed. She then became aware of Brunthe looking intently into the viseoscreen.

"Brunthe?" she asked.

"Yes, Mother?" he replied gently.

"What have you noticed? I cannot make any connection," she said in a disappointed tone. Brunthe continued to stare at the viseoscreen, walking closer to it with his chin slightly raised up, his hands neatly folded over each other behind his back, which itself was slightly bent over, peering intently at the images on the viseoscreen.

"Well, Mother, it's the child. Look into his eyes."
Mother replayed the viseo, zooming in this time on the child, rather than the dreadful image of the sister

wearing the dead officer's face.

"You see that?" asked Brunthe.

"I see everything, Brunthe," said Mother.

"Then see they boy's eyes. See what they say," said Brunthe, now in a reversal of roles - he was now the teacher, she the pupil. The viseo zoomed in closer and closer in an almost symbiotic sync with Mother's mind.

"I see terror registered. Paleness of skin indicates blood retreating to internal organs in response to shock, pupil dilation response is commensurate with-" this time it was Brunthe he who interrupted her.

"Recognition," he said simply, without over-emphasising the point. Mother paused. She thought. After some seconds, her 3-D image glowed a warmer colour and turned to him with a loving smile.

"You see, Brunthe - this is why I need you. Why you are so very dear to me. I know so much. Have so much information at my fingertips, and yet - there's-" Brunthe interrupted her again-

"More things in heaven and Earth than can be dreamt of in your philosophy..." said Brunthe, more to himself than directly to Mother.

Mother smiled and said nothing in acknowledgment. They both understood each other's limitations, and that they needed each other. They were placed together to make each other stronger. Their journey would always be together, at each other's side.

"Now - I have found it," said Mother - "Court Record 12943/xCevce. Let us watch, Brunthe..." Mother displayed the viseo record and they both watched intently.

Brunthe and Mother watched intently at the

viseorecord being replayed on the screen: Brunthe announcing to Mother that there is a legal appeal hearing scheduled; The Mother Board immediately leaving to allow Mother to make her judgement alone as they are not part of this process of the law; a woman and child being brought before Mother - standing in the darkness of the chamber with a cylinder of light displaying them like an exhibit in a museum.

"Ah, yes, Mother - I think I remember this - you allowed them to appeal against their tags, I recall," said Brunthe with some amusement. "Their barrister argued most strongly and learnedly - that it is against their human rights to never have their tags removed."

"And yet," said Mother, "everyone knows that you cannot have a tag removed. A most ambitious appeal, as you say, Brunthe."

"Audacious, even," Brunthe commented. Upon the screen, their barrister could be heard presenting the argument:

"The Mother and children have been tagged - and yet - although the mother freely admits her guilt - she was, after all, caught in a cellar, praying, part of a clandestine group soon appropriately and lawfully dealt with by our Faith Seekers, in her defence, only she - the mother - was present - and the children have never been to a meeting, have never been in any way influenced by nor-" Brunthe interrupted the viseo -

"They are always the same - always claim not to influence…"

"…was not introduced to religion and yet they too are tagged. In fifteen years they have been model citizens and yet - they should never be allowed to have their tags removed? Is there no mercy for those not directly involved in the crime? Porc!" The barrister shouted, looking as if he were to slam his hand on the table for

effect, before thinking the better of it when looking up to the giant hologram of Mother looking down on him. "P-O-R-C. *'Person of Religious Conviction'* he said with slow emphasis.

"Hmph. How amusing," said Brunthe, "he is acting as if addressing a jury - and yet he is addressing you - the originator and judge of all justice! It is most strange, Mother. I recall it clearly now." The barrister continued:

"This is akin to a Nazi concentration camp tattoo forever reminding them of the terrible things they had to endure - in fact, it is psychologically distressing because it is a constant reminder to the mother of the mistake she made in believing in religion - and a burden which is passed on to her children. She now wants to rid herself of that memory and get on with her life. Can Mother show compassion and clemency and, if not for her, then at least for the children, who have their whole life ahead of them, ready to give service to Mother and the journey - can she remove the tags and release them of this heavy burden?" the barrister's plea ended with sorrowful and heavy tone.

"Yes - I informed that that they would be released of their burden," said Mother.

"A clever ploy, Mother, of course," said Brunthe. The image of Mother's smiling face filled the screen as they were led out of the Mother Board. The viseo then displayed Mother's face becoming deeply troubled and saddened as she turned to the barrister, who is immediately held in place by viseobots descending and hovering around him with menacing hums of on-board weaponry.

"Ah, yes - there he is," said Brunthe. "Bradbury - what was it you ordered him to do, Mother?" he asked. As the viseo record played out, Mother reminded Brunthe:

"Yes - I asked Bradbury to interrogate the barrister - it was quite clear he was a part of the plot." Brunthe's face, at the sound of the barrister screaming, caused him to give an involuntary twitch in his right eye. Mother recognised his displeasure and turned down the sound from the viseo record. Brunthe turned from the screen, ostensibly to face Mother to ask a question, but also because he did not need to see the violence - the way FSO Bradbury effortlessly dragged the barrister across the proscenium and out of the great double doors of the Mother Board was enough to indicate would interrogation techniques would follow.

"And what did he find?" asked Brunthe; Mother made the screen go into fast forward, all recorded viseo comically speeded up. The violent interrogation recorded through Bradbury's viseocam was over in a few moments, but by the sheer terror on the barrister's face it was clear that that was far longer than most can endure.

"He revealed nothing - he had nothing to reveal - although a part of the plot, he had not been privy to any information. But of course, Bradbury then followed his instructions from me," stated Mother

"Which were?" enquired Brunthe.

"To wait and watch the mother and child. To lay in wait," Mother stated.

"The bait had been set," Brunthe mumbled to himself.

"Oh, Brunthe, you do yourself proud with your poetic turns of phrase - I learn much from you," she said, before continuing, "of course, I knew that whoever had wanted to find out if the tags could be removed would be waiting to find out if they had been successful. And so, Bradbury lay in wait. And this was the last communication session I had from him," she finished. Brunthe lifted his head to watch the viseo record being played on the screen. It showed the head viseocam, and a man entering the suspects' apartment. It showed Bradbury flying at the door - immediately smashing it to the floor and rushing into the room, before carefully surveying it. Bradbury held his gun steadily, calling out: "Faith Seeker! You will surrender!" With no response, Bradbury headed slowly for the next room - suddenly the lights went out and a figure flew from a shadow into the darkness of another room. Bradbury let off several rounds in a trail of the figure's movements.

"Mother - replay the scene in slow - single frame," asked Brunthe. Both he and Mother said the name in unison as a smeared and half-hidden face was caught for just a few frames. "Deacon," they both uttered. Bradbury entered the room; ordered his tag reader to scan -immediately two distinct tones bleeped, before its screen flashed the messages: 'Two Porcs present. 85th floor apartment, no escape.' He could be seen readying a flare but before he could activate it, the windows shattered through, the glass blown inwards by the howling wind outside. A figure jumped through the window and Bradbury ran towards it - immediately looking down he could see nothing - but above was the figure on the back of a sister hover bike accelerating quickly - he took aim with tag-detector bullets, but his arm was knocked to one side. He looked around to see the woman standing there. His tag detector could be heard shrilly warning 'Porc Detected' - her execution was an immediate reaction - one bullet through the head, which exploded, leaving her body drop to the floor. A scream could be heard, a scream of horror and desperation. Bradbury reloaded his gun and began to search. His sensors indicated breathing under the bed - he dropped to the floor and immediately aimed the nozzle of the gun - the laser locked - it was the face of a small boy, eyes streaming - choking with fear. He readied his gun, when the tag detector sent a message into his earpiece. 'Non-tagged human! Caution recommended'.

Bradbury looked carefully at the boy, he could see he was hyperventilating but it was too late - the boy's nose trickled a line of red and he passed out in fear. Bradbury lowered his gun, and reached in for the boy. Immediately, his legs were yanked backwards and he was dragged across the room - as he flicked his body around to assess the attacker, his headcam viseo caught the black and white of a sister looming at him, before going blank.

Brunthe pursed his lips as he turned from the viseo record to Mother's hologram.

"Two FSOs arrived at that moment, but it was too late for Bradbury - a drone was sent in pursuit but no trace could be found," said Mother.

"I see," said Brunthe - "And the boy?"

"Oh, he was still there; the Officers rescued him, of course - and sent him to Faith School, where he has been looked after ever since."

"Until today - when he was taken prisoner." Brunthe thought for a moment. "Hmm. I remember this incident. I vetted them thoroughly. That mother was genuine, I'm sure - her motive was genuine. I can't believe she tricked me," said Brunthe.

"Oh, Brunthe. She didn't trick you - you were absolutely correct. She was here in all sincerity and concern for her children. It was a real cause."

"Of course," said Brunthe, "Of course - the mother was utterly genuine in her actions and beliefs - a way of ensuring that she cannot be detected for lying or deceiving - she is a pawn, her utter conviction to convince us of her sincerity."

"Her whole life was that, Brunthe. Create a whole life for her simply with the purpose of finding out if a tag can be removed. It is a very useful weapon. Add it to our arsenal."

"Method noted, Mother. I must ensure to expand all checks in the future," said Brunthe as he added this tactic to the database.

"Thank you, Brunthe," said Mother. "Now, leave me for a while, Brunthe - let me calculate how best to proceed..."

16

Descent to the Crypt

Rome was cleansed. Seen as strategic to the demystification of the Euro Zones, its medieval and labyrinthine buildings and cellars had housed and hidden many religious cells. All had been cleansed, and to ensure dominance, a myriad of gleaming skyscrapers a mile high had been erected, and towered over the unseeing streets below. But once history has been buried deep into the ground, it is hard to erase that history from the consciousness of those who had lived there. Despite the danger, they felt they must return home, like salmon return to spawn and die, and start the cycle anew.

Atop one of the most impressive and technologically advanced of these skyscrapers, as it swayed with the force of the wind, sky bikes were buffeted as they tried to land and alight a small party. Making their way to an escape hatch for those on the highest levels, they waited a few moments; the hatch, bolted against the blustering winds, slowly opened, its heavy hinges ensuring a tight seal - but doors lead two ways, and through this door was a route into the building. The billowing black and white of two sisters stood sentry as the lift door closed. Inside this service lift, four more sisters, carried two metallic body bags and, leading them as in some parody of a funeral cortege, walked Deacon. Down, down, down the lift went, descending from the expanse of grey sky to the labyrinthine foundations of the building. As the lift reached the lowest point of its descent, the doors opened to reveal the service tunnels and areas which had been taken over by the Porcs - serpentine and dark, they were perfect for their purposes.

The metallic body bags were taken to rooms off the corridors where the smaller bag is taken into a room, a small cell containing a bed, before being roughly unzipped. With his nerves on edge, and the darkness heightening his senses, the sudden cutting whine of the zipper opening and the flood of light made Jude's eyes open in horror, but he is gently shushed by a sister: "Now now - here's a little something to help you sleep better. Everything will be fine." At which point she loaded a hypodermic syringe and injected him. Jude's eyes rolled, and he fell back into the deep darkness of the nightmarish visions locked inside him.

Watching his body twitch as if it were the jail of his convulsing soul, she looked satisfied, and said softly: "Don't worry - we'll soon get those demons out of you, my child." But those demons, once entered, seemed as trapped inside him as he was inside this building. No amount of convulsing and writhing could expel them. The sisters kept trying, and Jude kept crying. Crying and crying for his mother. He could see her so vividly, and no matter how many times he thought of her gently talking and smiling to him, the sisters seemed to have an ability to read his mind - and they would remind him - remind him of what he had seen. The Faith Seeker, with his black glove studded with metal covering her face, and the gun, so quickly pulled towards her head - but Jude's mother's eyes conveyed her message, and he turned his head away and hid as far back under the bed as he could. He heard the smash of the window, the explosion of the gun. And then, that Faith Seeker's face, lunging closer and closer to him, till it all went black.

Further up the corridor, in another cell, the larger metallic body bag was unzipped. The eyes here were wide open, not with fear, but defiance and surveillance. These were the eyes not of a victim, but an opponent. Sunetra looked to all corners of the room, reconnaissance her first instinct. Size, possible location, identifying features. Instead of the gentle lifting of the body which Jude had received, Sunetra felt two sets of hand lift the body bag into the air and tip her out into a heap on the floor. She felt a knee in her spine and, as her head arched back, and a blindfold was roughly pulled taught across her eyes, she saw, looming above her, the large wooden structure of a cross. Roughly hewn out of wood, it was clearly not meant for worship, but simply as a symbolic sacrificial tool; and for this purpose, it was equipped with ropes and spikes.

At the Mother Board, the chamber is illuminated only by the dais glowing gently, ebbing like the beat of a heart. There is a flurry of electronic activity inside the circle and the emblem of Mother, the laurel wreath, started to glow a vivid green. As the door opened, the slim figure of a man in plain grey clothes stood, waiting patiently. Looking into the dimmed room, as it become bathed in the green light the figure called out into the darkness:

"Mother?" he said. He waited; after a few moments, a plume of colours spread upwards from the laurel and formed into Mother's face - glowing, warm, smiling.

"Come in, Brunthe," she said. "I have been thinking. I have been wondering how to proceed," Mother said, her voice filling the chamber without losing any of its warmth or welcoming texture.

"What have you decided, Mother?" said Brunthe, who now phosphoresced in Mother's glow; there was a tone in his voice which did not indicate he was asking a question - there was no question - he simply wished to have his instructions. Whatever Mother had decided, there was no questioning it - Mother would be right, and her orders were to be followed. There was no question, no wonder. Simply a wish to receive instructions, which would be followed.

"I am going to take Mandrake and Constance offline," said Mother. Although there was no hesitancy in Mother's voice, no sense of wondering what would be thought of this statement, Brunthe felt curious enough to let an eyebrow almost rise.

"I see. What would you have me do?"

"Contact them. Tell them what I command. I will take them completely offline. They are to find Deacon."

"I see - because Deacon will lead them to Sunetra, and the prisoners, of course?" said Brunthe approvingly.

"Because Deacon will be at the nest. Find the infestation and they can stamp it out. Once they have found it, I will restore communication, bring them back online and they shall be given the full backup they will need to complete the operation," Mother instructed.

"Very well. I will ready a force and leave it on standby," said Brunthe.

"I'm glad you share the same confidence as me, Brunthe - Mandrake is utterly determined to find the nest. I have made calculations, and I believe that if he is left alone to do the job, then he will do it."

"Oh, I have every confidence, too, Mother. I have no calculations like you, of course, Mother - but I have a feeling," Brunthe said with conviction.

"Then that feeling is added to my calculations, Brunthe. And I feel even more confident now. Thank you, Brunthe," Mother said, glowing more warmly. "They will be rogue. They will have to fend for themselves. They will have to rely on their own abilities."

"Mandrake is a very experienced officer. And Constance is very proficient. I have all confidence in them. After all, Mandrake is very..." he made a small chewing motion as he searched for the right term, "Interpretive. Yes - he is very interpretive of orders, so acting rogue should be quite believable for our enemies, and quite within his abilities," Brunthe said, and then gave a little nod of satisfaction. "Of course, once the infestation has been dealt with, we will have to decommission both of them?" Mother glowed, and affected a sadness in her voice:

"Both Sunetra and Mandrake will have to be immediately decommissioned – I will send the order to Faith Seeker Constance to eliminate them once their work is done."

"And Brunthe said that to you?" Mandrake asked with a note of incredulity in his voice.

"Yes - he came through on the viseocreen - he said our orders from Mother are-" but Constance was cut off by Mandrake.

"To go rogue - no communication - do what we have to do - without backup, without orders?" he asked.

"We have orders. We will have backup as soon as we request them," said Constance with a little exasperation.

"But if we are offline, then how are we supposed to ask for backup?" said Mandrake. Constance ignored this and carried on stocking the drone with food and water.

"Look - Mother has ordered us to find the base. Let's get that done. Then, when we get there, we will find a way to signal. I don't understand why you are having such difficulty in following orders. Don't you want to find the Porc nest?" asked Constance. She looked at Mandrake. He was looking up at the shattered sky of the Faith School, continuing the conversation as he looked determinedly at the gaping crack of the sky.

"Of course I want to find it. We have to rescue Sunetra," he said with fixed purpose in his voice.

"FSO Sunetra? She could be dead already. I think the priorities are straightforward - Mother's instructions are to find the nest. We set that as Goal One, of course. From the evidence of the viseos we can see that there are prisoners taken - some children and adults. We rescue all prisoners, if possible, provided that there is no compromise to Goal One."

Constance sounded very matter of fact, working out the strategy as they were loading supplies. But as she was rushing through the varying strategies her training had enabled her to do, there was one aspect which she felt was absent - she felt alone. Always Faith Seekers are bonded together - their single pursuit of the goal was always prioritised and the feeling of esprit de corps always ran through them. But this time, all her strategies, possibilities, and sifting through altering scenarios were strangely unanswered. She felt alone. But as she glanced as her side Mandrake was right there next to her. Her mind started to wander. Even when she was left in a solo position, in the middle of a nest, imminent death at her heels, she always felt near to everyone - one word over the comms and the reassurances and advice of her fellow Faith Seekers would embolden her and reassure her that she was not alone. As she was stacking the shelves with food, she glanced at the life systems computer on her sleeve: it confirmed Mandrake was standing right next to her. She could hear his breathing and feel his body heat, and yet, she knew not why, she signalled the computer to scan for life around her. She darted her eyes towards Mandrake and then entered the sequence. It was a strange physio response in her body as she waited for the scan. Despite her facing death and pain on hundreds of occasions, of witnessing and being subject to horrors that ordinary people would never recover from, she felt a flicker of anxiety cross her heart, like the miss of the beat as it readies itself for conflict, she felt the wave of adrenaline rush through her and even - she searched around in her mind for the words to describe it - fear. What was it she feared, she wondered to herself. She realised that she had a feeling that Mandrake's life signals would not show on the computer - that it would state that his life signals were not present. That with the signals of non-existence lighting up on her screen, she would find herself in the presence of a ghost. Constance jumped as she was startled by the triple bleep of the computer on her wrist.

Before the bleeps had finished, Mandrake had hit the floor, drawn his gun and was shouting for Constance to cover. She immediately knelt and drew her gun - both of them pointing towards the door of the drone. Mandrake whispered:

"Signal coordinates?" to further narrow the point of attack. No answer - he glanced over to Constance to see her staring at the life detection computer on her sleeve. "Where is the life?" he whispered with more command and urgency. "What has it detected?"

"You," said Constance softly, and lowered her gun. She stared at the readout. All life signs normal, two people. "I must have left it on by mistake, after we were scanning the school. I must have forgotten and then when it detected you, I wasn't expecting it," she stammered unconvincingly in her explanation. She was surprised at her sudden ability to make up lies quite easily, to try and cover herself, which caused her further confusion; Faith Seekers did not lie - there was never a need to, unless it was strategic, but she found it quite easy.

The strong, gloved hand of Mandrake covered the computer on her sleeve and she felt him crush it till his fist encircled her entire wrist - she looked into his eyes, and then the computer cracked and popped and arced as it was destroyed by the crush of his fist - but he stopped before her wrist felt the force in an exercise of control. He kept his fist locked around her and said: "I need you to be on top form for this mission. If you're malfunctioning I'll leave you here and do it myself," Mandrake said with a slow and steely determination in his voice. She met it with an equal determination of her own. She was a Faith Seeker - and she was his equal.

"Mother needs us for this mission, FSO Mandrake. And I am ready to follow her orders at maximum efficiency." She looked at her wrist held firm by Mandrake, and he stared at her intently as he relaxed his grip and let her arm fall. As it fell, so did the crushed computer drop to the floor. Mandrake crushed it further under his boot, to ensure its destruction. He stared at her as he stamped down on it.

"We are now offline. There's no Mother. There's no one else. It's just me and you." He flicked a switch and the doors slammed shut, and the drone's engines started to whine and rise with increasing tension.

17

Rescue Mission

Slowly moving over the city, matt black and almost indistinguishable from the dark grey clouds which cloaked the skies, the drone hovered like a bird of prey over open fields. And like a bird of prey, its eyes focussed on the tiny movements far below, darting back and forth, waiting for a patch of grass, or bush, to give away the hiding place of the target. The cityscape of thousands of tiny flickers and movements each triggering a response, before being dismissed as irrelevant. Inside the drone, Mandrake watched the buildings and the streets. Cameras zooming, screens showing body heat signatures, electrical use, data zones, electronic cross-talk - all manner of different tools designed to flush out those who hide. Being a Faith Seeker drone, no clearances were needed, no questions were asked, all permission were automatically granted. All other air traffic gave way and swiftly changed routes to accommodate the drone: no one would dare to interfere with Faith Seekers at their work.

Constance opened a nutrient pack and passed it to Mandrake. She ate several in anticipation of needing the energy.

"Scanner says your blood sugars are getting low - ketones detected on breath analysis - your body is starting to use its reserves. You'd better eat now, before we go in," she said. Mandrake did not reply but simply took the protein bars and ate them methodically whilst watching and running further scans over the city.

"What makes you think they are here? In this city?" he asked.

"You make me think that," she said. Constance meant it - she didn't know why, but she just had a confidence in him. She somehow knew that, despite him working by instinct on several occasions, that he would always back this up with scientific knowledge.

"Look, we followed them to this city by tracing their heat trails-" said Constance

"The heat trails from the sky bikes were almost evaporated by the time we left - we shouldn't have wasted time stocking up," said Mandrake with a measured amount of blame-putting on Constance.

"And so we locked-in on the pollution trail from the bikes!" countered Constance.

"Which was fast dispersing in the wind-" continued Mandrake before again being interrupted.

"Look, Mandrake. If you have better information, knowledge or experience to share, then tell me when it's relevant - not as some stick to beat me with after when it's too late. I don't understand - we are Faith Seekers - we are dedicated to working together for the same cause - but I'm getting the impression that really, you're on your own. You're not working with me - I have an uneasy feeling about this and I might have to abandon the-" but Mandrake talked over her:

"Do you want me to drop you off?" he said with an eagerness which irritated her.

"No. Mother has given us the mission. To accomplish it we work together - or I go back online and inform Mother." Mandrake stayed silent, continuing to look at the scanner screens.

"Mother had faith in us - something she knew about us made her decide that we were the best Seekers for the job. And Mother is never wrong. So what do we do about this?" Constance, she felt she was wavering a little, that the very act of thinking about Mother's decisions was intrinsically wrong, and that she had already crossed a line which should not be crossed. Mandrake turned slowly in his chair, away from the screens, and looked directly at her.

"Well, Mother certainly knew about which ones to choose to go rogue - you're questioning her already." Mandrake had no malicious undertone to his voice – he was simply stating fact.

"'Mother is never wrong'", you say, and yet you are trying to understand why you think she made a mistake-"

"I didn't say that!" interjected Constance sharply, her eyes darting around, senses on full alert. "I was merely-"

"Relax. We're offline. Mother can't hear you," Mandrake said with an invocation to his voice. An invocation to something beyond Mother. "I know how you feel. It's a very strange, heady feeling to be offline. We are bred, reared, trained, and educated our whole lives to be the physical manifestations of Mother's will. She can always hear us - always!" said Mandrake with some urgency.

"No she can't. There are times when she can't," said Constance.

"That's right. She can't, but she can. She doesn't because she doesn't need to. Because you do it for her!" said Mandrake in a tone which seemed to make everything lucid, while actually disguising the paradoxes.

"I don't understand," Constance said with a gentle tone which she was unused to. It made her feel like she was back in the gendarmerie, learning with all those other thousands of boys and girls, rows and rows. At first, she had been afraid, but soon, she would learn to control that fear. And as she bonded with the others, she soon learnt to use fear as a whetstone to sharpen her claws for the kill.

Mandrake spun his chair back to the screens momentarily, and ordered the navibot console to keep the drone on a straight course and continue scanning. He walked over to Constance and told her to sit down. She did, with a slight hesitation, and then he sat opposite her. They talked quietly, reverentially, in the dimmed lights of the drone. In the background, the whine of the engines rose and lowered in pitch in rhythm with the gentle turns and lifts of the drone, like a bird of a prey as it hovered and tilted, watching, searching. The flickering of the myriad lights on the consoles cast shadows and tones across their faces as they talked, morphing their images from one perception to another.

"What is it that you want?" asked Mandrake, simply, sincerely. Constance was aware of herself blinking - she looked at Mandrake and his angular face and square jaw altered from strong and fierce to gentle and welcoming as the different lights bathed his face in different colours -

amber and red, then blue and white. She stared, and then a series of bleeps and flashes in the ceiling made her look up, a little startled - she thought for a moment that Mother could hear her - jolting her out of her reverie:

"I want to exterminate all Porcs, to wipe out all religious belief, to make this world safe-" Mandrake interrupted the rehearsed phrases coming from her mouth.

"No - that's what Mother wants," he said firmly.

"Don't you want that?" said Constance, a little alarmed.

"Yes. I want that. We all want that. We all-"

"We are all on the same journey. We are all working together. Walking together. Marching together. We want-" again Constance was cut off by Mandrake:

"We are. But some of us want to take a different route." Constance felt a jolt. 'A different route'. This sounded like heresy. Constance could feel her muscles in her arm and hand twitch with anticipation, and her mind started planning the route and body movement her arm would take to reach her gun, draw and fire it into Mandrake's brain. She tried to hold his gaze while planning it in her mind but he was quicker than her. Mandrake had seen the signs - the subtle eye-movements and the lack of concentration on the subject. When he saw the corresponding twitches in her hand he acted without hesitation - in a fraction of a second Mandrake had her gun in his possession - she immediately went to seize it, to grapple it back out of his fist - but for all her strength and agility, she was not able to match his powerful grip - she could see that he was ready for combat, and she could see that he would win. She just made one more twist of her arm as an act of defiance.

The gun let off a bullet which hit some electronics in the ceiling, sending a blue crack of electricity and a shower of sparks towards them as the ship to lurched to one side. Mandrake kept himself steady and held her arm locked.

"It's Ok," Constance said, "I'm not going to do anything." Mandrake let go of her arm and put her gun inside his uniform. He ordered Constance to sit back down as he checked the systems on the drone.

"Hull damage. We're losing oxygen and heat. We'll be fine," he said, sitting back down opposite her.

"Look. Constance. Mother is never wrong. I know that. And I'm as dedicated to the cause as you are. But we only have one life, and-"

"We don't have one life - our life is Mother's. We are born to serve her. We serve Mother and we serve the cause!" said Constance, rapidly going into a syntactical propaganda roll.

"Ok, Ok. We have a mission to do - let's do it. The sensors are showing a stronger heat patch on the hull - go and check that bullet hole - see if there's anything you can do." Mandrake was back in mission mode. Constance went over to the patch where the electronic circuits were still sparking. She put her helmet and visor on as a protection against the electrical sparking, then stood on the console to get a better look. Carefully placing her face close to the ceiling, she could make out the small circle of the bullet hole. A few stray wires betrayed a clean breach of the hull. Constance put her head as close as possible to see if the hole was ragged or could be patched up. As she did so, she noticed the shaft of skylight penetrating the hole suddenly being blocked out. In its place was the swivelling and jerking movement of an eyeball. She jumped back in astonishment, losing her balance and falling off the console.

"There's someone out there!" she shouted, clawing at her empty gun holster. Mandrake jumped onto the console but the hole now only displayed a shaft of light. He ran over to the computer and ordered the outside cameras on. Swooping away from the drone, leaving a plume of black smoke, was the sinister outline of a sister on a sky bike.

"Follow the heat trail!" shouted Constance, running over to the naviconsole and taking charge. Mandrake pulsed the engines to full power and the drone whirred wildly as it lurched before powering downwards towards the city, the sensors locking on to the heat trail left by the bike, which swerved and weaved wildly in evasive action, going low, and zigzagging in and out of the skyscrapers. The drone was unable to keep up with the manoeuvrability of the sky-bike in these confined spaces.

"Go high!" shouted Constance, and Mandrake took the drone back up to a level above the city. Constance adjusted the sensors and watched carefully. "There!" she said with satisfaction. She pointed to the image on the screen. "That building there - it went on to the roof." They set the drone on its course, and lowered it gently down on to the top of the skyscraper. They could see on the screen the sky-bike's heat trail under a metal canopy. There was no sign of the sister, but the detectors showed her foot fall towards a door. Mandrake put his hand inside his uniform, took out her gun and handed it back to Constance.

"Thank you," she said, before looking directly at him and saying: "Remember - Mother's not here for us - we need each other."

"That's what I've been trying to tell you," said Mandrake as they readied to leave the drone.

18

Trial by Ordeal

Sunetra moaned deeply. She had not regained consciousness and yet the pain was so deep inside that an autonomous wail of pain welled out of her. She didn't know what he had done to her. It didn't really matter. This flesh of hers was not hers. It was created as a sacrifice. A sacrifice to Mother. And she was more than happy to die for her. After all, she had done what she had been born for. Achieved all that could be asked of her - and so much more. How can she give any more? She felt there could be no more to give.

"Mother...Mother...Mother!" called out Sunetra, unconsciously at first, until, becoming aware of herself calling out, she emerged into consciousness again. She had no idea how long she had been under, or what had been done to her. As her eyes cleared, through the blurred penetration of light formed a face. It was the face of Deacon. She could hear his voice, with its unsuppressed tone of impending violence.

"Mother is not here. She has abandoned you. She

has given you to me. She does not care what I do with you!" said Deacon with a salivatory relish in his voice.

Constance and Mandrake looked carefully at the lift. A lift was always a potential trap. It was never a good idea to enter a hostile territory with all your officers trapped inside a box with one exit out to the hypothetically waiting enemy. No guard, thought Mandrake. Just like an invitation.

"What would you do, in their situation?" Mandrake asked.

"Well - I would warn everyone that they are here," she replied as she looked at the lift floor indicator - it was waiting at the top level. "Either they've been down, and sent the lift back, in which case they are waiting for us at the bottom, or-"

"Perhaps they don't even know we found them," said Constance. "They might not even know we are here."

"That's a distinct possibility," said Mandrake. "Ok, you go down in the lift, and then send it back to me if the area is safe," said Mandrake. Constance looked at him incredulously.

"You expect me to go on my own?" she asked, her gaze steady at his. He broke away, answering:

"We go together." They readied their guns and pointed them at the lift door. Constance pressed the 'door open' button'. They tensed themselves. The door slid open to reveal a narrow emptiness.

"Ok. I don't think they know we're here," said Mandrake.

"I thought so," muttered Constance. They walked into the lift, keeping their guns ready as the doors closed. From around the other side of the pillar, the black and white figure of the sister moved out of the shadows and stared at the lift as it descended to the depths of the building.

"Now - you tried to do the worst possible thing that can be done to a man - to take away his faith. Now it's my turn - I'm going to take away something of yours. Sunetra started to mouth the standard responses learned in her training,

"Mother knows where I am. They'll be here soon…" she mumbled like a talisman, "they know exactly where I am…" With an expression which showed Deacon's impatience for someone who he felt was misguided and would not learn, he smiled, and moved his face close to hers:

"Mother does not know where you are. She has made you learn these words by rote to give you false hope. She wants you to sacrifice yourself for her in the hope of a false belief. Mother does not know where you are, Sunetra. If she did - I and all my brethren would be dead by now. They've no idea where you are!" he whispered, his pouted lips brushing her ear. Deacon moved his position to the front - facing her squarely, obstinately. Again, he moved closer - until he stood with his mouth breathing into hers.

"You see," said Deacon, "I have The Lord on my side - and with that comes powers bestowed on me by Him - powers which you do not possess - nor can hope to, unless you let him into your heart. Will you let him in to your heart?" Sunetra gave no response. "Hm. I'm going to have to take a little look in a minute - see what the heart of an unbeliever looks like. I wonder what colour it will be? Black, I expect. Anyway - don't worry

- I'll show it to you, too. Non-believer look in on yourself - that's what the bible says - and I will make sure you see right in!"

"My heart is not open to a non-existent being-" started Sunetra, before her vision became black and flashed with the light of a blow to her head.

"Don't insult Him in His own house! Have you no manners? He, in his infinite glory, has given me powers. Where you questioned me, tried to dissect and classify me through your sciences - which did not work - I - through the Lord - have his permission to dissect you. You are an animal. And we use animals to dissect for research." He put his face almost against hers - "You are my dog!" He meant it as an insult - and he was surprised at the flicker in her eyes. Almost as if she were insulted. As if she cared. "My lab dog."

Deacon moved away and looked at a tall object which was standing some feet away, but opposite to Sunetra; whatever it was, it was the height of a person, but was draped with a purple cloth to hide it. Deacon looked back and forth between the two, hoping that Sunetra would show some interest. Finally, he plucked the corners of the cloth with both hands, and lifted it with an extravagant flourish, like a magician revealing his best trick; it was a full-length mirror.

The reveal was disappointing to Sunetra - he could see it in her face. He was angry at the lack of appreciation she showed, but then understood the problem. For her full appreciation, she needed to be able to see her reflection, and the angle was wrong for that. He stood behind the mirror, and deftly, slowly positioned it in front of her, ensuring he never took his eyes off her face. He turned it around with a slowness that demonstrated how much he was enjoying this - staring intently into her eyes to glean as much pleasure as he could.

Deacon had cut her open so deeply, delved inside her so much - and it had given him so much pleasure, and yet, strange as it may seem, he thought, he felt that somehow he was penetrating deeper into her by looking into her eyes. He did not understand it. He just knew he enjoyed it and it gave him pleasure. It was just another of the mysterious gifts from God that he was thankful for.

Sunetra stared into the mirror as its angle turned and glinted towards her - and she was caught by her own face in its reflection. All she had wanted to do was to protect the thing inside her. Her flesh she would give. She would happily sacrifice that. But not that thing inside her.

As Sunetra swam back into consciousness again she focussed on the mirror - she was used to seeing these sorts of sights, of course, she had supped on horrors since she was a child - Mother had ensured she was prepared from a very early age. But it did catch her attention more when the flesh ripped apart was your own. Her eyes darted and focused to see better. Deacon, staring at her, gave a smile - he could see that she was suddenly aware of what she was looking at - that she was aware of the horrific carving he had performed on her body - knives cutting deeper with lunged slices, the delicate clipping of tubes followed by the tug of clamps and the peeling of sinews. He didn't know what they were, of course, he had no idea - it was a strange fascination to him - all he knew was that the deeper he cut and ripped, the more pleasure it gave him. He was very proud of the two large stainless steel clamps which now held her open. The glint with which they displayed the colours of her inner organs with the glistening steel was somehow pleasing to him – his work was magnified and highlighted so well - he suddenly shouted, as he saw Sunetra's eyes clouding over as she fell into unconsciousness again – he was angry and was feeling deprived and cheated.

"Sister, why is she slipping away from me?" he demanded through venomous tones. Sunetra's head lolled to the side and she was surprised to see not a sister dressed in black and white habit and cowl, but the face of a woman much the same age as her, looking carefully at her. Sunetra went under again as she heard the woman apologising:

"I'm sorry, brother - this is very difficult -" she was cut short by Deacon's voice.

"Sister, my own clever sister - one of the best surgeons we have - and you cannot perform a simple procedure to -" he stuttered in his frustration and fury.

"It is not simple, brother. If you do not want me to give her any anaesthetic or pain relief at all, then I cannot stop her passing out. It is a simple chemical response. All is in the balance, brother." Deacon's sister tried to placate him. At the side of the cross on which Sunetra was tied were drips and banks of blood, with their tubes feeding into Sunetra to keep her alive and replace the blood constantly oozing from the open front of her body. Deacon's sister tried again to soothe him.

"Let me give her some pain relief - just enough to keep her conscious - not to help her, or ease her pain, but to increase your pleasure? If you want her awake, she cannot feel the full extent of her wounds - it is too much - even for a Faith Seeker." Deacon was convinced.

"My beloved sister, I have full faith and trust in you. Bring her round - do what you have to do - just wake her for me. She has felt all I have done to her - it is now important that she sees it, too." Deacon's sister started administering various drugs, and within a few minutes, Sunetra was moaning again. Deacon's sister took hold of her chin and shook her face, gripping tightly:

"Faith Seeker! Faith Seeker! Wake up! My brother has much more to give you!" Deacon stood directly in front of her, the mirror facing the ground and reflecting the pool of deep red expanding there.

Sunetra coughed and spluttered, and opened her eyes. She breathed very deeply, acutely aware that her body was short of oxygen. As she opened her eyes to the light, she realised once again where she was and what had happened. Deacon resumed his taunting:

"Look, Faith Seeker! Look what I have taken from you!" He slowly angled the mirror, and looked voluptuously into her eyes. As the mirror turned, Sunetra could see her stomach held open by two large steel clamps. He eyes feverishly looked into the cavernous opening there. Deacon smiled - she was looking with utter disbelief at his work, he thought, she was in the depths of despair and horror, he thought. Look at the way her eyes will not leave the mirrored image of her own body's violation, he thought. But Deacon thought wrong. Inside Sunetra's mind, her thoughts were very different.

She looked into the image and felt inside herself. She was astounded. There was a revelation, an epiphany inside herself that was both exultant and joyous. She stared deep into the mirrored reflexion of her own mutilation - and though he had opened her insides to their full extent, and exposed all that was there - he had not found it. The Thing. The Thing inside her was still there. She stared into the mirror, but it could not be seen. But she felt inside herself. And the Thing was still there. He had not found it. It was still safe inside her. And she cried with relief and smiled as her head once more lolled into unconsciousness.

19

Cross Examination

Deacon carefully traced the tip of a large knife around sleeping Sunetra's face, deftly following the lines and contours.

"Brother - I can see you find her face...fascinating," said Deacon's sister, with a hint of disgust. Deacon did not look away from Sunetra, but instructed his sister:

"Do not ruin her face. I want to keep it afterwards."

"Why this one? We have many Faith Seeker faces for the sisters to wear," said his sister.

"I will keep this, for-" he turned slowly to look his sister in the face, "for pleasure," he said, smiling at her. Deacon's sister knew what this meant, and gave him a weak and submissive smile to acknowledge his request before turning away.

"Now - bring her back to the world of the living - I am ready - the force of God is in me, and I am ready for her," said Deacon with relish. Deacon's sister went to one of the tubes in Sunetra's arms, opened a valve and then filled a syringe of clear fluid, before attaching it to the tube and dispensing it into the catheter with a steady push.

Sunetra started to moan and move her head from side to side. "That's it. That's it," said Deacon. "More - give her more!" he said with a rising voice.

"It's a difficult balance - one mil too much would kill her," said Deacon's sister with real concern - to deprive her brother of his pleasures would mean severe punishment for her.

"Keep her alive - I have a lot more for her yet!" Sunetra moaned and opened her eyes as the second shot of fluid coursed through her veins, her pupils dilating wildly, unable to focus. Deacon took her chin in his hand and whispered into her face, ensuring his breath entered her mouth forcefully.

"God says I have not penetrated you deep enough. He has talked to me, Sunetra, while you rested, he has talked - talked directly to me - about you! You are very privileged. He says, if I penetrate deeper I might be able to reach inside and find the last vestiges of humanity in you! I might be able to touch your soul!" he shouted into her face, spitting. "I might be able to save you! He screeched triumphantly. "What sort of a person would I be if I didn't even try? His voice lowered from maniacal edginess to one of personal concern, and tenderness: "It's going to be hard, hard for both of us - but we have to try," he said, effusing camaraderie, breathing heavily into her face.

Deacon's sister turned her face away, ensuring he did not see any signs of disgust registering in her expression. She always had to stay and witness these things - and it was always women. The men could never be saved, for some reason - they were always beyond redemption. But the women, the women he would never give up on. And she would always have to bear witness.

"It is my duty, Sunetra. My duty to try and reach inside you," said Deacon, bringing the knife tip up and circling it around the open wound of her stomach. She flinched, causing the clotting blood to start to flow and plasma to weep again. Through the haze of her unfocused pupils, she could see that he smiled at this, at the oozing of the fluid from her open stomach. Deacon's sister noted the pleasure on his face - it was time to ready more drugs to prolong the ordeal.

Seven sisters stood, weapons at the ready, for the lift to finish its descent into the crypt. The numbers flashed through their sequential pattern, before suddenly stopping at the midway point. The hoods turned to each other, faces inside the darkness unable to fathom the reason for this. Minutes passed and their agitation started to show – a further two sisters checked again that the cage behind them was ready - an iron cage rusted with the blood and gore of previous inhabitants, its medieval appearance in keeping with the crypt's architectural style. Two of the sisters swung the iron doors of the front open, and positioned the cage against the lift exit. They waited, and then, after a few moments, the lift numbers started to descend again.

In the dimmed and yellowed space of the crypt, the lift dropped to the bottom of its depths, and signalled its arrival with a single bell note. Nothing happened. The sisters waited, and nothing happened. The bell rang again, but the doors did not open. At a command, the cage was pulled back from the door, and two sisters stood at the entrance with guns ready. Another, signalling the others to be ready to spring, pressed the door open button. The doors did open, and the candles flickered and staring back at them were the four steel walls of the empty lift - their own warped reflections staring back at them. Disbelieving, the sisters crowded round, all wondering how the two Faith Seekers had disappeared into thin air. The bell kept ringing in a receptive mocking of the fact that the lift had arrived, but was empty. One of the sisters pulled back her hood to get a clearer view, and as she did so, she noticed the back wall of the lift distort her image like an old fairground mirror. The back wall of the lift was held in place by the tips of black-gloved hands at each end. And between the fingers of each hand was a nozzle. Before they could react, lasers pulsed from the nozzles, punching a hole in the clothes of the habits of the sisters, before setting them ablaze with the intense heat, before the garments crumpled to the floor with the incinerated sister inside.

Before the remaining sisters were able to return any fire they were all smouldering on the floor. The back wall of the lift wobbled, and it fell to the floor with a metallic twang, leaving Constance and Mandrake standing there, surveying the bodies for any signs of life. Stepping over them, Mandrake said:

"We stay together at all times."

"Understood," responded Constance. She placed a substance over the 'door open' button, keeping it ready for their future exit, the bell ringing periodically, echoing down the corridor.

"Once we have located them, we make contact and inform Mother, right? Go back online, and signal Mother?" Constance whispered.

Mandrake, nodding, adding: "Yes - but we have to establish that this is the actual nest, and then try and rescue our officers first, of course".

"I think we've already established that- we could go back up now, and find a way to signal…" said Constance, but Mandrake was not listening. He was entering stealth mode, performing reconnaissance of the area and moving forward, one goal in mind – to rescue Sunetra.

Sunetra breathed deeply through her nose, oxygen was essential, and she could sense her falling levels as the blood loss continued. Every time she stopped breathing hard, everything in the room started to swim again - colours and sounds melding into a nonsensical blur. The drugs being injected into her were keeping her alive, and preventing their administration was an option she had ready.

"Do you take him into your heart?" asked Mandrake with an even, intense and robotic tone.

"You will not be able to reach me," she mumbled, "they are on their way. Very soon you will all be dead," Sunetra murmured drunkenly.

"No one is on their way, Sunetra - you are on your own. I can read you - read you like a book. Every twitch of your face - every sigh on your lips - they are all words to me. I can penetrate right inside you. I have penetrated you - while you were unconscious - you know that. I've had a little look - I can see I'm not the first one - our brothers have been there already, I see? But I will penetrate you so much deeper than them. I have to – it is God's will - it's your last chance for salvation. I will go past your heart - and deep into your soul," said Deacon.

Sunetra stared at him, her focus moving in and out with the dilation of her pupils.

"You gave the order to kill hundreds of innocent children. You murdered them in cold blood. Defenceless children. How can you live with that?" said Deacon, but it was not a question in any rhetorical or actual sense - the emphasis was on her acknowledging her guilt – of making a confession.

Sunetra was struggling to make any meaning of what was going on around her - the mutilation, torture, lack of oxygen and primordial pain was a combination her body could not bear much longer. Deacon's sister, reading her body responses on the monitor, could see this - no matter how much more she administered medicines this person would slip into unconsciousness and soon die. She signalled to her brother; he nodded and Sunetra felt the large soft outline of an oxygen mask pushed against her face. She breathed deeply, giddiness engulfing her, her head feeling as if it were splitting with the surge of oxygen back into her blood stream. Images began to coalesce and she began to feel more of a sense of where she was. Her consciousness was rising.

Deacon faced her, and suddenly gave the clipped and precise tones of someone making an official announcement:

"I have looked as hard as I can. There is nothing there to be saved in this person. They are possessed by the devil and there is no possibility of saving them. They are already past saving. The Lord has given me orders - she must feel the pain that she inflicts on others." Sunetra wondered what was to come - any more torture and she would be dead – she had to buy time before she was rescued – she knew that Mandrake would rescue her

– she just had to hold on.

"I carried out a command - those people were executed because they were convicted terrorists - Porcs are to be exterminated-" said Sunetra with regained vigour. Deacon snapped orders:

"Silence! The devil talks with forked tongue. Seal her mouth and bring in her loved one. We shall seek the truth from them."

Suddenly, a gag was pushed tightly into her mouth and tied round her head. Sunetra was puzzled - she looked around as people started to set up cameras and take positions around the room. A door opened, and her eyes widened in horror and she started to moan and flail. Two sisters were dragging in a small cross - tied to it with rope, it's legs bound tightly, panting in horror and pain, was a dog - Sunetra's dog. The secret she had kept for so long, the touchstone of solace she went to for a few fleeting minutes of love and pity and joy - her secret was discovered and brought before her in mockery of her own tortured body.

"Here, boy. Come on, boy!" said Deacon, calling to the dog, but looking at Sunetra, "come to daddy!"

20

The Disappeared

Sunetra was crucified. Her naked body was spread-eagled on the cross, her eyes were closed, and her head lay to one side in a reposed and peaceful image which belied what had happened to her. Her eyes had fallen, lit gently by candlelight; her face was still, the only movement the from the flickering of the flame; once again the candlelight gave a series of subtle flickering – it was enough to rush adrenaline back into her bloodstream. Sunetra's eyes suddenly opened wide with conviction. They darted searchingly around the room. There! It happened again. A uniformed spluttering of the candle light - enough to rouse her to the possibilities. He was coming; she was certain of it. She needed to prepare herself. She was counting, of course. Counting the seconds. Three minutes between each flickering. He was going through doors, she thought. Going through doors, floor by floor, de-alarming, defusing, clearing a pathway into the depths, and securing an escape route.

Sunetra could see her torturers in the corner

discussing, planning, laughing - safe in their beliefs. She glanced over at the cross to which they had tied her dog. It was covered in a sheet, but it flickered and twitched - he was still alive - she was sure of it. There was a slightly more noticeable flickering of the candles - enough to make Deacon aware and look up. The others looked to him. The souls of the long dead fly about these crypts, they said. The living guard every level, every floor. They are safe. Another flicker. Again, three minutes before each one.; the pattern was there. Sunetra readied herself. She watched Deacon closely. He said he had to go to the toilet urgently, pointing to his stomach - he shouted:

"Are you sure I've not been poisoned?" accusingly at one of the guards. He told his sister to "keep an eye on these - I have to go to the toilet. I may be some time." Sunetra's interest was triggered. He knows, she thought; he knows. He's read the signs just as I have and he's getting out. She watched him move, carefully taking his things with him, subtly, so as not to arouse suspicion; she saw him look carefully around - he barely glanced at her, he had lost all interest in her now. He was just ensuring his own safety. He went towards the doorway, then with a sudden movement was invisible amongst the shadows.

Flickering; flickering. Six minutes. Then nothing. For a moment, Sunetra's heart kicked hard inside her - what if Deacon knew? What if he had gone and found Mandrake? What if Mandrake were dead? She calmed herself. Control. All she could hear now was the heavy, fast breathing she was emitting. The blood loss was still continuing - she must not put any more strain on her body unnecessarily. Flickering, quite strongly. A candle blew out. He's hear, she thought. Was that something?

In the shadows by the main door? She looked intently before becoming aware of a heat by her left cheek. Smouldering - she moved her eyes slowly to her left side. The rope which bound her wrist was smouldering under the glow of a laser. Non-vis spectrum... She kept her hands very still. The right wrist was now subjected to intense heat. Sunetra kept still and kept her nerve. Both her hands were now free. Suddenly, Deacon's sister stood up from her chair:

"What's that burning smell?" she shouted. She looked down to see something roll under their table - her mouth open to say something - Sunetra bent herself in half, touching her toes to minimise the exposure of her body - the pain through her open stomach was too much to bear and she had to scream. It did not matter, however, the scream was absorbed by the screams of the others as the light grenade went off under their table, an arc of green light forking and jumping between all organic life within its area.

Deacon's sister's mouth lit up emerald green as the electricity sparked across her teeth. She slumped smouldering to the floor, her hair crackling as it shrivelled under the heat. The guards who were still alive at the table dragged themselves towards their guns - one lifted up a burning arm and pointed his pistol at the black figure which formed out of the smoke - he momentarily saw a red flash from the figure before feeling his arm explode in a tangle of sinew and muscle.

Within a few moments, all life seemed to have left the room save for two - two people whose hearts beat ascendingly as they held each other. All their training, their survival techniques, their skills, were forgotten as they fought to hold each other and melted into each other's arms.

"It's now," whispered Sunetra, "It's now. I've had enough. We have to do it now. I don't think I can live…" Mandrake nodded his head in acknowledgment of her wish. The time was now. Their allegiance to Mother was over. They were now their own free spirits.

Mandrake carefully applied a large clear wound pad to her stomach to stem the blood from spilling more, picked her up and carried her across the room. He shouted across the room:

"Administering Medicare - give me cover, Constance!" Constance shouted back acknowledgement, bursts of machine gun fire punctuating her speech. Mandrake untangled and removed the tubes connected to Sunetra, and administered some injections of pain relief and anaesthetic from his own Medicare pack. Sunetra tried to override her body's desperate need to slip into paralysis - she must first be safe, and then she can let herself go.

"Mandrake- my dog," she begged. Mandrake was incredulous, but followed her line of gaze and her wishes without question. He walked over and lifted the sheet to look carefully, before Sunetra was at his side and pulled the sheet away in desperation. There, on the cross, was nothing but congealed blood. Sunetra stared before being startled by a moan, a gasp of humanity - Sunetra dragged herself over to the sound:

"We have to go, Sunetra!" said Mandrake urgently. She walked over to Deacon's sister, who was still smouldering on the floor, her hair melted into the skin of her face. Sunetra lifted the woman's head so she could see, and then pulled a scalpel out of Mandrake's first aid kit. Deacon's sister gave a smile - she knew what Sunetra was going to do:

"Take mine," she said. "I want you to have it. It's a gift." The building was suddenly shaken by an explosion, the coffins rattling their contents on the stone shelves.

"Just one minute!" said Sunetra, rifling through the medicare equipment scattered across the floor. She found a sealable bag, and looked back to the table with the array of scalpels and medical tools.

"Just give me one minute" said Sunetra. She didn't look to see if Deacon's sister was dead yet - her eyes were focussed on her stomach, and she lifted the woman's top.

Constance burst through the door, shouting "Down!" They all dropped to the floor as the grenade she had thrown twisted the metallic frame of the door, sealing the corridor behind, and them inside.

"Porcs in force outside. There's no way back to-" she suddenly interrupted herself when she caught sight of Sunetra's helmet discarded on the table. She ran over, trying to activate it; it was unresponsive. She quickly ran to Sunetra, who was sealing something in a bag.

"Activate it! It's our only hope!" Sunetra looked at Deacon, he gave a nod.

"FSO Sunetra - activate and connect." The laurel wreath glowed an olive green and the instruments lit up inside the helmet –

"We're online!" Shouted Constance - she went to grab the helmet to call for help, but Mandrake stopped her. A voice came through the comms pack.

"Confirmed contact - you are online, Sunetra - position and state?" asked the voice - Mandrake took the helmet and spoke into the comms pack:

"Building location grid ref 398627.4464. Crucible building-" the helmet instantly responded:

"Located - Faith Seeker response drones on their way - find a safe place and maintain-" but Mandrake cut the voice short:

"Two Faith Seekers down," he said, "Mandrake and Sunetra. Both dead. Beyond repair. They can't be saved." Constance stared at Mandrake, unable to comprehend the meaning of his words.

"Who is this?" queried the other officer. Mandrake looked at Constance, and proffered the helmet towards her. She didn't know why, but she said what she thought they both wanted her to say:

"Faith Seeker Constance here - going back online with FSO Sunetra's comms pack - I confirm the two officers are dead. Awaiting backup." She felt stunned that she had collaborated in this deceit.

"We need to go now," whispered Sunetra.

"Yes," Mandrake replied, "We need to go now. The drones will be here in a few minutes, and this whole place will be incinerated," he said.

"Way we came in is sealed - we'll have to blow it open and fight our way through!" said Constance, already preparing explosives.

"Going to be difficult with Sunetra down - we need to find a way to get out without conflict-" Mandrake stopped talking as a female voice from behind them said quietly:

"I know a way out. I'll show you - if you'll take me with you?"

Atop the skyscraper, their cowls and hoods billowing in the savage wind, two sisters stood guard over the hatch, silver machine guns aimed and primed. Behind them, huge ventilation fan, the blades standing 20 feet tall, swirled with such force it seemed they seemed to inhale the very clouds above them. The fan started to slow, slow until finally the blades came to rest with reverberating tone like wounded animal. The sisters turned to look, and were astonished to the black silhouette a Faith Seeker slip through the blades and fire a laser directly at them. Still conscious, they could do nothing but fall to the floor and writhe as the laser beam melted holes through their spinal cords. As the figure delivered two bullets to their heads to ensure a safe path, more figures slipped through the huge fan blades. A teenage girl led the way, followed by Mandrake, Sunetra held tightly in his arms.

Constance and the girl made their way through the howling wind towards the resting drone. As they approached, the doors slid down and Mandrake ordered them to keep guard while he took Sunetra on board. He came back to the open doors, lifted his gun and pointed it at the girl-

"Wait!" shouted Constance, "What are you doing?"

"She is unknown. I'm not taking a risk," he replied.

"I'll take the risk. She got us out alive, didn't she?" stated Constance. The girl, no more than a teenager, edged closer to Constance, looking naturally to a protector.

"Ok. Move away from the door. You can look after her," said Mandrake.

"You're not doing this, Mandrake!" said Constance with fury, drawing her weapon and aiming towards Mandrake. The fact that he hadn't immediately killed her the moment she went for her gun gave the reassurance that he did not want to kill her if possible.

Mandrake did not put the gun down, but kept it levelled at her. He suddenly looked up into the sky - approaching them were dozens of drones, lights blazing in the distance.

"We haven't got time, Mandrake! Let us on board!" Constance shouted. Mandrake calculated that they had less than a minute to escape. Sunetra's voice called down the gangway:

"Let them in," she said, "let them join us if they want." Mandrake lowered his gun, and the girl and Constance approached. "The comms pack," ordered Mandrake. Constance threw Sunetra's helmet to the floor, and Mandrake immediately destroyed it with a single pulse of a laser. They both boarded the ship and Mandrake readied the ship for emergency take-off. As they strapped themselves into their seats, the door hatch raised to seal itself, but before it could, the black and white figure of a sister left to guard the drone hauled herself up and into the craft.

Mandrake pulled the throttle to full power, and the engines whined complainingly as the drone rose from the building and lifted off the roof to hover in mid-air next to the building a mile up. Mandrake suddenly cut the engine and the ship plummeted in free-fall towards the city streets below. Steering it like a glider, he flew it using gravity for as long as possible, desperate not to leave a heat or engine trace for them to follow. He tilted and swerved it through buildings, precariously swaying as the ground rose nearer and nearer. On the scanner screens could be seen streams of people leaving the emergency exits to the building, flowing out and into the city, merging with the others till they were indistinguishable and untraceable. How many were Porcs, and how many innocent citizens they could not guess. They heard the explosions and fire of the drones as they raided the building - there would be no mercy shown. With the ground now precariously close, Mandrake powered the engines again, and the powerful pulse pushed the hurtling ground away from them, their stomachs pulled with the gravity-defying arc of the ship. Once Mandrake was sure they had not been followed, he headed the drone back up and into the sky.

"Where are we going?" asked Constance.

"Hospital - you are admitting Sunetra-" Mandrake informed her.

"They'll never believe that - she's got rid of her uniform-" replied Constance.

"We are your prisoners - Mother has instructed that Sunetra is an important Porc and she wants her life saved. You tell them to put the womb back-" he said.

"The what?" asked Constance, with complete disbelief for the second time that day; she felt at a loss to understand all of this. Mandrake, stepping into her personal space, pointed steadily towards the sealed bag:

"Her womb," he ordered - "you tell them to put back her womb!"

An explosion rocked through the crypt, shattering the long-dead bones and crumbling the stones which had held them for centuries. Through the chocking dust dozens of Faith Seekers streamed into the crypt, killing those who still showed signs of life, searching for information and acting as the eyes of Mother.

"Over there - cover and check!" called one of the FSOs over her intercom, wary of booby traps. She looked down and switched on her viseo feed for Mother. The two bodies huddled by the blood-stained cross seemed to be those they were looking for. Two bodies in FSO uniforms, one female, with her stomach cut open and innards removed, her face burnt beyond recognition, the other male, with one arm blown off at the elbow. The officer looked carefully at their badges - the names read 'Sunetra' and 'Mandrake'. The officer lifted his scanner - it bleeped at the bodies, then flashed vigorously, the screen message blaring 'PORCS DETECTED.'

Mother's voice came over the comms to the officer, ordering him to take DNA samples, and further photos. Mother's voice seemed to have a slight irritation to it, thought Brunthe, as she said, looking over the pictures pixel by pixel:

"Those bodies are not theirs. They are not Mandrake and Sunetra."

"It makes me wonder why they bothered – they know we can identify their bodies no matter how badly damaged," said Brunthe, "Perhaps they just wanted to buy time?"

"I think not, Brunthe - it would have taken time to attempt the deceit - preparing these bodies, dressing them in their uniforms - no, Brunthe - they wanted me to think they were dead. They wanted to be forgotten," said Mother.

"What on Earth are they playing at?" wondered Brunthe, with the slightest tone which betrayed worry. Mother's hologram swooped around and faced Brunthe:

"Do you have a theory, Brunthe? If so, then please share it with me…" she said.

"Well, I've noticed, in Sunetra, that is, I wonder if…

I'm not sure, Mother, I just wonder why they would want to escape," he said with consternation.

"Escape? said Mother, "That is not a pleasant term to use – they are not prisoners, Brunthe!"

"Indeed, they are not," he replied, "I just wonder if they… if they…" Brunthe seemed to not want to say it in front of Mother, so she said it for him:

"If they care for each other. I, too, Brunthe, wonder…" she said quietly. Brunthe then wondered aloud:

"It's almost as they are in love…like they are human."

Around the skyscraper, people watched from the safety of the city as Faith Seeker drones pulsed up and down, picking off air bikes as sisters tried to escape. Guns, lasers, explosions - all manner of weapons were used and the people of the city marvelled at the ruthless efficiency and skills of the Faith Seekers as they pummelled their way through the building, floor by floor. On giant viseoscreens across the city, Mother transmitted messages in her loving, soothing addresses to the people:

"This infestation will be cleansed - our Faith Seekers are hard at work - rest assured not one Porc shall escape to spread their terrible infection…" Gazing up at the huge screen images of Mother, a man and his teenage child sighed, then turned and disappeared into the multitudinous crowds. The boy looked up to the man, asking:

"De-"

"Father!" The man quickly corrected him - "Just for now, till we are safe," said Deacon.

"Father - are you sure we can find her? My sister - I

can't believe she is still alive - I'm sure she would not have gone with them freely - she would have fought to the-"

"Death?" Deacon finished his sentence for him - "Oh, yes - she would have - she told me she loved you very much - and all she prayed for was to be reunited with you - her one surviving sibling! Oh, yes - she fought - but they are very strong, the Faith Seekers - and very evil. To take her hostage to aid in their escape - cunning! Look," he said, and showed a hand-held screen. It showed security video from inside the building, and the girl could clearly be seen surrounded by the armed Faith Seekers, being led through the corridors. Jude watched, and the anger built until the images showed the girl standing on the roof next to the drone, with one of the Faith Seekers pointing a gun directly at her head before she was ordered on to the drone; the anger tipped into hatred.

"But - do not fear, my child - I have this!" and Deacon pulled a device from his pocket - a Faith Seeker tag detector - and upon pressing the button, it lit up with his sister's name 'Karma'. "When we can get near enough - it will lead us to her - and then you can be reunited!" declared Deacon with a large smile. They disappeared into the crowd, hand in hand.

21

The Promised Land

The damaged drone sped fitfully from the city, dropping low over the ocean, its engine pulsing erratically, belching black smoke before firing again, dropping so low that the crested waves sprayed upon its sleek outline. Inside, Mandrake sat at Sunetra's side, mopping her brow, caring for her with a tenderness which was incongruous in a Faith Seeker. Constance looked on quizzically - absorbed by the show of affection and care between them which was not part of her medicare training; the meaning of their behaviour made a thought form inside her which made her uneasy, her mind erratically echoing the drone's vicissitudinous journey. She became aware of the girl motioning next to her, calling her name hesitantly:

"So - you three are Faith Seekers, right?" she asked, with some fascination in her voice. Constance nodded. "Cloned killing machines made by Mother?" Constance nodded again; the girl looked over towards the tender tableau presented by Sunetra and Mandrake, and quipped: "Just checking." She got up and walked towards them, asking:

"Is it Ok if I come near?" There was no response so she carefully made her way over and looked pitifully at Sunetra. "She looks really bad - he did terrible things to her in there. He likes to do that sort of thing. I usually put my headphones on so I don't have to hear," she said, becoming more prone to talk the less Mandrake responded. She paused for a moment, before asking: "Do you think she's going to be alright?" Mandrake turned slowly, looking her full in the face.

"I'm going to make sure she is. We have a long journey ahead." Hearing this, and seeing that he was now ready to answer questions, Constance asked:

"What is this journey, Mandrake? If you want me in on this I have to know everything - it's standard procedure to be fully briefed before any..." she stated insistently until her words died away. Mandrake looked back over his shoulder towards her:

"We don't want you in on it. You wanted in on it - both of you!" he said, glancing at the girl. "This is for us. Sunetra and me. I don't mind telling you, but if you don't want to come, then I will have to kill you both," he said flatly. The girl gave a little nervous laugh and looked towards Constance: she suddenly realised that it was not a joke - Mandrake's intention was just that. The girl thought for a moment, then asked Constance-

"What do you think? We could be dropped off at the hospital - we could walk away and that would be the end of it." Constance gave no affirmation - she wanted to know what it was they were doing, and turned to Mandrake again:

"Ok - Mandrake - tell me what's happening - I want

to be a part of this." Mandrake never turned his gaze from Sunetra, who slept fitfully under the drugs he'd administered.

"We are going to a hospital, Sunetra is going to be made well again, and then we are going on a long journey. We are going to the promised land," he said simply; there was no response. He lifted his head and looked at them before saying more firmly: "We're going to The Idyl!" Constance and the girl looked incredulously at them, before the drone lurched further, and continued in its inexorable descent from the sky.

In the heat and smoke of the engine room, breathing in the leaking fumes in the filthy air, a hooded face was suddenly lit up in ghoulish green as a transmitter screen faintly bleeped in to life. The sister hovered at every word she could hear - and the mention of The Idyl made her lick her wizened lips with the intensity of the secrets she would reveal to Deacon, ready to transport the stolen secrets back to Deacon the moment she was able to fly again.

Now feeling underwhelmed and cheated, Constance and the girl vented their frustration:

"It's not real! It's not a real thing!" said the girl with broad incredulity in her voice, before Constance joined her in support:

"Mandrake - The Idyl is not real - and it's not for us! It's what Mother has promised for the people once the world is rid of all religion. Our job is to make this world ready for The Idyl-" she was interrupted fiercely, intensely, by Mandrake:

"It *is* real. It is a place. It exists now! And Sunetra and I are going there - and no one will stop us!"

"But how can... How can you know? How can it be

real? Mother has said we are working towards it - and Mother does not lie," Constance said with conviction in her voice.

"I've told you what I know. It is the truth," said Mandrake. The girl looked at Constance for a response, but was met with a blank. The girl, however, burned with questions.

"Look," she said to Mandrake, "we can't just follow you - not with no evidence... with just your word to rely on!" she said in a rising voice of incredulity. Mandrake said nothing, but there came a weak voice rising from Sunetra:

"I believe in him. I believe in The Idyl. If he says it is real, then I believe him. If you want to follow him - then you must believe in him too," she said before lapsing back into unconsciousness. The girl suddenly stood up, galvanised by Sunetra's words:

"I believe you, Mandrake. I believe and I will follow you to The Idyl. Please - take me with you," she asked. Mandrake, though still tending to and watching over Sunetra, without turning his head, asked the girl her name.

"Karma," she said, "My name's Karma." Nobody said a word, but there was an implicit sense that everyone was waiting for Constance; somehow, she picked up on this, and, without knowing why, her allegiance formed into words:

"I believe you, too. I will follow you to The Idyl," she said falteringly.

Back at the Mother Board, these words crackled over the speakers, broken and dissected, but with enough to allow Mother and Brunthe to understand. Brunthe phosphoresced in the intensity of Mother's glow - so bright and fierce it might be mistaken for anger.

"I have nurtured and raised them as my own, to be obedient and truthful to the cause, and they have betrayed me - their own Mother," she said with a heavy heart. "Why are they doing this, Brunthe?" she asked, though Brunthe knew it was not for him to say, it was a question more rhetorical than entreating. In a few moments, Mother answered it herself:

"It is a failure in their upbringing. I will instruct Genetics and Education to review their Faith Seeker production processes. They are putting the future of humanity at risk." Brunthe nodded suppliantly and waited patiently for the orders he knew would follow:

"Deploy Faith Seeker Torque," she continued. "He is to eliminate them all, and all those they have come into contact with - their words, their ideas, their bodies must be wiped from the face of the Earth!"

Printed in Great Britain
by Amazon